DEPARTURES & ARRIVALS

AN ANTHOLOGY OF SHORT STORIES

Edited by
'Doc' David, Sarah Jones, Peter Meinertzhagen,
Sarah Milne Das & Tiffany Williams

Oxford Writing Circle.

DEPARTURES & ARRIVALS
An anthology of short stories

First published by Oxford Writing Circle Press in 2020

Text & art copyright © Individual contributors
Cover design © Alexander Walker
< www.alexander-walker.co.uk >
Illustrations on pages 31, 55, 69, 76, 125, 134, 166 ©
Sophie Temple
Book layout: 'Doc' David

A CIP catalogue record for this book is available from the British Library

ISBN paperback **978-1-9998832-4-9**
ISBN ebook **978-1-9998832-5-6**

© Oxford Writing Circle Press 2020

CONTENTS

Dear Readers,

It is our pleasure to introduce *Departures & Arrivals*, the fourth anthology of the Oxford Writing Circle.

We were once described as Oxford's most democratic writing group, and it's a review we're especially proud of as it encompasses who we are and who we want to be. More writers are joining us; at the time of writing (October 2020) we are coming up to our sixth birthday and have nearly 1,200 members on Meetup, the site where we began. We frequently see new faces at our feedback sessions and writers' brunches, and older members called away by other things are always welcome back.

We're also a diverse group; not only in who we are but in how and what we write. We, the editorial team, set the theme *Departures & Arrivals* hoping writers could take it in ingenious directions, and we were not disappointed. In this anthology you will find a time-traveller on a mission to undo the past for a car crash victim; the secret thoughts of a maker of sugar glass for movie stunts; the funny side of expecting your first baby, and much more.

We would like to take this opportunity to thank everyone who contributed their writing and art to the anthology, and everyone who helped make this publication possible, including our editorial team, our illustrator Sophie Temple and our cover designer Alexander Walker.

Finally, we thank you for picking up this book, and hope you enjoy reading it.

Here's to the future!

Sarah Jones, Peter Meinertzhagen,
Sarah Milne Das and Tiffany Williams, 'Doc' David

DEPARTURES & ARRIVALS

AN ANTHOLOGY OF SHORT STORIES

DESTROYER OF WORLDS

Isabel Galwey

Her name's Lin Park, and she's a destroyer of worlds.

That's what she tells herself on mornings like this, anyway, when she's had one too many margaritas the night before and she's feeling slightly worse for wear. 'Lin,' she says. 'You. Destroy. UNIVERSES. For a living. Now get out there and show the commuters what's what.'

She's just downing her first coffee of the morning — and wondering whether using the Loom to go back in time and take back that fatal third cocktail would get her fired — when her iPhone rings. Lin winces at the noise and checks the ID. *Ugh* — it's Kerri from reception. What does she want at this time of the morning? To rub in the fact that *she'd* managed to avoid the temptation to get shots last night?

Kerri starts talking before Lin can even say "hello".

"I'm pushing back all your meetings for this morning, and don't you dare complain. That famous singer — *you* know, the one you're always listening to, the one who was in a motorcycle accident this time last year — *Lin,* he just came in the door! Here!"

A stupid little buzz of adrenaline hits Lin's stomach. "What — Jack Lee?"

"That's the guy! The one whose eyebrow game was a meme

back in 'twenty-five."

"I, um, wasn't here for that."

"Oh yeah, different timeline, I guess that one didn't make it through. Anyway — you'd better get here fast, Lin. Otherwise someone else'll snap up his case."

"How do you know he — "

"Oh come on, don't be stupid, Lin! Get your arse *in* here!" She hangs up.

Lin stares into the mirror. "*Destroyer of worlds*," she says to herself again.

As she sits on the tube she gets out her Kindle and starts to read. The train judders and when she looks up, she spots a middle-aged man eyeing her Kronos lanyard with a mixture of admiration and horror. He glances away, trying to rearrange his features. It's funny to think that what she does for a living scares him, although perhaps it's not surprising.

When the tech had first come in, of course there'd been an uproar. The lawmakers had worked around the clock. The Vatican had released a papal bull debating the immortal soul's durability across timelines. The Nobel Prize suddenly hadn't seemed big enough.

"We are now approaching King's Cross Saint Pancras," an automated female voice intones. Lin will be back here later on today. No, not *here,* she needs to remember that. But somewhere so similar as to be indistinguishable.

The Kronos Corporation owns a big building right at the centre of London, in that glassy dead zone where the property prices seem to lack any connection with reality. Kronos started out in Lagos, but when the founder realised she'd hit the jackpot, she took her operations global. They catered to governments, to movie stars fallen from grace, to terminal cancer patients — anyone who had a few millions of dollars to burn. Good or bad, composed or wretched — all of humanity came in through their doors. From Manhattan to Dubai, from Rio to Seoul... The business grew tenfold overnight, and Lin was one of the hurriedly trained-up new recruits who came to work at the London office.

"Please take care when leaving the train." Lin blinks and stands up in a hurry. A few more seconds and she'd have missed her stop.

As she steps onto the escalator she yawns massively, then winces at the too-loud chatter of the schoolboys behind her. She needs to start getting more sleep, she tells herself; she's not a student any more, she can't roll out of bed at noon. She stops off at the station Caffe Nero (fancy that, yesterday it was a Costa) and buys herself a double-strength mocha. She sips it with only minimal guilt; she's earning enough that she can afford to treat herself to little things like this.

Fresh out of Cambridge, with what she called a 'passion for quantum theory' on her CV, Lin hadn't hesitated when Kronos came calling. The only thing that saddened her a little when she started time-travelling full-time (as it were) was how little one universe differed from another. The specials at McDonald's might be Mex rather than Tex, and it was fun to see kids playing on Tamagotchis in the really old timelines, but fundamentally, nothing much changed. And of course, there were laws about going to see cool things like dinosaurs and Hitler.

"You're in," Kerri announces, grinning, as Lin walks into the office. "You'll be seeing him at ten. Good luck."

Lin smiles, then drains the last dregs of her coffee, the joint caffeine-sugar rush starting work its magic. "Cheers," she replies. "I owe you one."

"Don't let me forget it!" Kerri calls after her.

Over the past few hours, there are a few things that Lin has learnt about Jack Lee.

One: unlike most celebrities, meeting him in the flesh isn't a disappointment. He's objectively handsome: dark skin, hazel eyes, the famous eyebrows; and a smile that looks like he's never worried about anything in his life.

Two: This smile is deceptive, because the year before he'd had a very awful, near-fatal accident, followed by a very public mental breakdown. And yet, to look at his face, Lin can hardly believe that he can really want this.

Before he pulled his chair up to the desk, though, she'd glimpsed his legs, obviously shrunken despite the baggy jeans, as well as his crabbed left hand, strapped into place on the wheelchair. His other hand, smooth-skinned and short-nailed, is tapping a pen against the desk. Along the inside of each wrist is a pale pink, jagged scar.

"So, before we go through to the Loom, we need you to sign these papers," Lin says, trying to keep her voice cool but friendly. She pushes the heavy stack over to him. "Then you'll need to go through a one-hour "cooling-off" period and a final check that 12th June 2029 is really the date which you would like—"

"Is this really necessary?" he asks, very pleasantly, but with a slight tensing of the jaw. Three: he is understated. Slight movements are as close as he comes to expressing his desperate impatience, bubbling away below the surface. "I don't want to wait much longer," he adds, levelly.

"This isn't just about you," Lin says, going for a note of severity. Kronos has enough leverage over their clients — even the powerful ones — that she doesn't need to worry about sugarcoating things. "Quantum collapse is no small matter. If you knew the amount of energy required to transfer currency across timelines, not to mention the extrapolation needed to make sure that our alterations are comprehensive —"

Jack holds his hand up in a pacifying gesture. "Okay, okay,

I get it. It's chill. So — I gotta come back tomorrow? To get it done?"

Lin sits back too. She feels irritatingly flustered. "Well, you don't need to be there, actually. But we're just making sure you know... We won't proceed into the Loom for another day."

"What, so I just — go home? Seems a little... anticlimactic."

Lin gives a tiny sigh. What was he expecting? To walk into a white light? "My apologies. Kronos likes to keep things functional. Don't worry, your new reality will match the old one perfectly. There might be a few cosmetic differences, but there's laws which mean we can't alter anything major, even if we wanted to."

Jack eyes her steadily. "There are some people who believe this whole thing is just a massive-ass hoax. My friend Nicky said I should've just... saved my money."

Lin meets his gaze. "By definition, nobody can witness the collapse of the universe." She bites her lip. "But let me assure you... It's definitely real."

There's a beat of silence, and then Jack away, the corners of his mouth tugging down in an expression that approaches pity. "Okay, Lin. If you say so."

No matter how many times Lin uses the Loom, she's always stunned by its beauty.

It's a huge chamber filled with pulsing, infinitely refracting rays of light in every imaginable hue. The space is pleasantly warm, balanced between the thrum of the generator and millions of industrial strength fans. She wonders what it must have been like to be part of the original Kronos team, working through the heat of a Lagos summer, getting spliced and mixing timelines and going mad, some of them. Her mouth feels dry, and she longs for a cold beer.

In the end, it's not difficult to find the spot. Routine. Longitude 39, latitude 56, not too far above sea level. She fires up the machine and puts in her headphones, tries to forget about the infinitesimal chance of splicing. It gets easier every time.

When she opens her eyes, she's standing in a little market town, listening to the woosh of traffic. It's mid-morning, 12th June the year before. Jack has just arrived back at his country house after his latest sell-out Europe tour. That evening, some of his friends are coming around for a party. They'll have a few drinks, then one of them will suggest getting out the motorcycles.

Lin checks she's got everything. ID, old-style banknotes, quantum flare for emergencies. She rents a car using cash and a fake name, then drives to Jack's house. She bangs on the door three timesconfident, authoritative.

She's just about to knock again when Jack opens it. He looks sleepy, relaxed, a little confused — she's a stranger to him now, after all. Lin blinks, hard. She always finds this part difficult — the moment when she sees her wretched, broken clients whole again. The moment before disaster.

Jack's starting to look confused, so she takes a breath and composes herself, extending a hand. "Hello, Jack — I'm Sonya, Trish's new PA." She hands him her Universal Records ID card. It's authentic; that is, provided by the studio. "I'm *so* sorry to tell you this but you really need to come back up to London this evening. It's an emergency."

"What's up?" he says, sounding just slightly annoyed. He'd warned her he'd be difficult to budge.

"Someone's threatening to leak some photos of you to the tabloids —" she takes a deep breath and then says it — "some photos of you from your ex-girlfriend's phone."

Jack *yelps* at that, and Lin resists the urge to sigh with relief. Even after months of experience, this part of a job always stresses her out. "How did — what did you —"

"Get in the car right now, there's no time to explain. Needless to say, Trish is *not* very happy with you right now."

Jack scowls but does as he's told.

They're crawling around the M25 when Jack smacks his forehead. "Fuck! I didn't tell Jerry and Nicky that I wasn't gonna be —"

"No need, Trish has already called them for you." Untrue, but it doesn't matter.

Lin bites her lip, deliberating. This isn't part of her job description, but she can't help it — she wants to say *something.* "Jack," she says. Stops, steels herself, starts again. "Jack — you really, *really* need to start being more careful. With your photos, with your motorcycles... Everything."

Jack's starting to frown slightly, which, for him, is the equivalent of turning purple with rage. "Hey, um — Sonya, was it? — I don't really know you, so I don't know why you're —"

"— Please just listen! You don't want to end up cutting short a really amazing career just because of some stupid decision you made when you were drunk,' Lin interrupts, and she's surprised to discover how much she means it. Her voice is shaking slightly. 'You don't know how quickly it can all fall apart. How easy it is to just — it really doesn't take a lot, Jack."

Some people have it coming. Murderers, abusers, corrupt politicians... Oh, they always express remorse, they always cry and storm and promise, but Lin wonders — how far would you have to turn time back to make someone really change? Oh, of course, she keeps tabs on them in her new timeline, remembers names and faces and crimes. But she still wonders.

Jack isn't like that, though. He's a bit silly, a bit feckless, but Lin's met enough bastards to know that he's a fundamentally decent person. He deserves to live a good life, and a long one.

He deserves *this*.

Now he's glancing at her sidelong. He almost looks impressed. "Nobody talks to me like that any more."

Lin tightens her grip on the steering wheel. "Maybe they don't dare. Or they just assume that you won't listen."

Jack doesn't reply, choosing to stare out of the window instead. Lin hums a tune. He glances at her sharply.

"That song hasn't been released yet," he says, slowly.

"Oh, I guess — Trish played it to me earlier," Lin lies smoothly, though inside she's cursing herself for making such a rookie mistake.

Jack looks puzzled, but shrugs. Lin glances down at her watch. One hour until the moment of the accident passes; and then, after that, she can clock out. She'll drop him off at Universal Records, leave before he can ask any questions, and then head over to Kings Cross. It's a standard Loom rendezvous — public, solid, dependable. Universes may rise and fall, but so far, Kings Cross remains. And so does Kronos.

A few hours later, the car rolls up — its number plate simply reads 'K-2030' — and once again, Lin knows for sure that Kronos is still standing in this timeline. As always, she can't quite decide whether she's relieved or disappointed.

The PR department at the London office is lobbying to use blue phone boxes instead of cars for their pickups. They think it'll help to boost recruitment. The thought makes her roll her eyes. Then she gets into the car, leans back in her seat and waits.

As soon as Lin walks out of the Loom, she pours herself a very stiff drink. Gin, and then a little tonic as an afterthought. Nobody bats an eyelid as she cracks open the can. She's not the only one in the office who needs something to help her unwind at the end of the day. Far from it.

"So, where have you been today?" Kerri asks. She's filing her nails.

"Oh, I was saving this singer Jack Lee. He was got in a motorcycle accident last year." This particular case isn't redacted; the client didn't do anything incriminating, just stupid. It's nice being able to talk about her day for once.

Kerri looks gobsmacked. "Wow, I didn't even know that he motorcycled. He just got engaged in this timeline, actually."

Lin smiles. "Glad to hear it." She adds a few pieces of ice to her drink, then pours another for Kerri. "I owe you," she says, handing it over. "You made sure I got the case."

"Really?" Kerri smiles vaguely. "That was nice of me."

Lin gives a forced laugh and changes the subject. "What's on the agenda for tomorrow, then?"

"Oh, we're cleaning up some huge police brutality scandal that blew up in Stratford," Kerri sighs. "Bit less glamorous, I'm afraid. You'll meet the clients tomorrow morning."

And this is how it always goes. Get spat out of one flawed, collapsing universe, straight into another. And this one wouldn't last long either. By tomorrow, it would be gone, too. None of them would feel it. That's what Kronos always said, anyway. But a painless death is still a death — the end of a timeline, something that no longer exists. Nothing except for a few million pounds sterling, and Lin Park.

She looks out over the city and takes a sip of her drink. She listens to the faint rasp of the file across Kerri's nails. They're are a different colour here, pink instead of blue. Lin thinks back to that doomed world, to Jack's mismatched hands. To his wrists with their pale jagged scars.

She sighs. "Hey, where do you want to go out tonight?"

THE END

OPEN MIC NIGHT

Carole Scott

Good evening, ladies and gentlemen, what a nice-looking audience you are. My name's Cherry McFarlane and I'm a serial dater. Well, I was. I've recently resigned my membership of the 'nation of swipers.' No more left and right for me, folks. I'm clearing the wreckage of the car crash that was my dating life. Anyone single here? Question for you — how have we become so addicted? It's not as if it's fun. My average swipe session goes something like this: mid-life motorbike, look at my fish, six pack, dick pic, beer gut, golf. I see a few women nodding their heads; you know exactly what I'm talking about, ladies.

I've been going at it a year, which I think deserves a medal. Time wasted that I'll never get back. Could someone please just tell men to ask a few questions? I know you're nervous, boys, but you're sitting opposite a live human being, not a blow-up doll.

Oh, you'd prefer a blow-up doll, would you, Sir? At least you're honest. Maybe we should fix you up with a coma patient from the hospital — at least it would be a warm body to hold at night.

Back to the dating farce. Ever had that pump of anxiety when you accidentally swipe right in panic when a colleague's face pops up on screen? Nearly put me off right at the start. But I battled it out.

First up was '65p Steve,' the penny-pinching dentist, who took five minutes to calculate his — cheaper — share of the bill. 'Not-a-chiropodist-Chris,' the pedantic podiatrist, whose hour-long answer to *what do you do?* gave me more knowledge of the connection between hips, knees and foot troubles than a medical student on rotation. Then sweet, quiet John. A missed lunch and a second gin and tonic meant I started off loud and got louder. He didn't call again.

I think 'Closet Colin' was next. A serial entrepreneur, a bit older, a twinkle in his eye and beautifully turned out. When he declared his love of the ballet, I was thrilled and jokingly replied, "are you sure you're not gay?" He didn't kiss me at the end of the night and I never heard from him again.

Proceedings with 'Hedge Fund Harry,' a fast-talking New Yorker, got off to a rocky start when I asked why rich people need a fund to manage their hedges. Surely, they can afford gardeners? No, no, don't groan — I babble when I'm nervous. Once he recovered from my dodgy attempt at humour — yes, mate, I know all my humour is dodgy — once he recovered, he was charming. He liked my big brown eyes and lively smile. I began to think that a kiss at the end of the night might be welcome.

What I didn't know was that Harry's 'love of travel' had soured like warm milk when his wife fell for Bart, the yoga teacher on their Maldives getaway. When I said that travelling brought out the best in me, I wasn't prepared for the volley of anger that cracked across the table.

"What IS it with you women? You can only relax and 'be yourselves' when you're somewhere out of the ordinary."

I bristled a teensy bit at that point. But I'm British. You know what we're like. Fizzing with fury inside, polite and smiling on the outside. I'm not sure who didn't call whom. Let's agree it was me.

Oh, and 'Vile Victor,' who started the evening by asking, "Are you a good kisser?" And who later halted a conversation about politics to size me up and declare, "yes, you do have good legs, don't you?" He seemed surprised when I left.

I did have a lovely six weeks with Josh. He was intense and I was flattered. I bet some of you know the type — deep in, quick out. No, I'm not talking about the sex. That — since you ask — was glorious. Two weeks in, he whispered: "This relationship is going to be amazing! We're going to be so good for each other." I casually suggested that a whole weekend together would be lovely, but "no pressure because I know you have the children and lots of shifts at the gym."

Foolishly, I imagined that he would arrange for his ex to have the children, not straight away, of course, but within a few weeks, maybe. Nope. We carried on seeing each other once or twice a week, always at mine. I plucked up the courage to ask him whether he was married and cheating. He stormed out and didn't return my calls.

I plunged straight back in. 'List-lover Luke,' who took twenty minutes to name every gig he'd been to in the past year and didn't return the curiosity. Then 'Dodgy-tunes Dave,' who cited Chris de Burgh, Shania Twain and Maroon 5 as his top three music influences. I'm not proud of myself but I deployed the 'friend with an emergency' line.

Speaking of friends, mine loved all of this. I swear I got invited to some dinner parties just to be the entertainment for the night. Chilled white or rich red, the seasons may change but the welcome stays warm when you have fantastic dating disasters to share. All but one of my friends are coupled-up (some married, others engaged or close to it), so they surfed on the vicarious thrill of dating jeopardy, safe in the knowledge they didn't have to venture out again — well, probably not until their mid-50s when divorce will surely come along to smite some of them. Confession: every time I came home from one of these dinners, I felt happier talking to my knitted elephant than I had all evening. Well, it chips away at you, doesn't it, having to be funny when you're lonely as fuck. Sorry, got a bit deep there. #LightenUp Cherry.

I bet you're wondering what brought on the sudden end to my swipe-tastic adventures. Warning, you're about to find out how quickly I lost my British Politeness.

Oh, I haven't told you what I do. Critical information. I wanted to be a doctor but I didn't get the grades and dropped out due to a burning lack of ambition, so I became a pharmacy assistant instead. It's not a bad job. It's regular hours and I'm building up a lot of material — you don't get to deal with prescriptions, piles and the public without having stories to tell.

What does pharmacy have to do with dating, I hear you ask? Well, okay, you didn't ask but I'm going to tell you anyway.

It started with a Rich Tea biscuit on one saucer and on the other, a Jammy Dodger and a chocolate Hobnob. You can see what's wrong with this picture right from the off. There was no balance, no harmony. Had the single biscuit been a homemade shortbread or a crisp ginger snap, a quirky asymmetry could have been argued. However, this was a café, not a canvas, and a date for two, not a still life, so the fault wasn't one of aesthetics. It was one of manners.

Gary grinned at the waitress and turned back to me, saying, "I'm a regular, so I get special treatment," before scoffing both luxury biscuits at speed. A first date, you're trying to impress the girl, and you fail to mitigate the uneven biscuit distribution situation. Do you ask the waitress for a second biscuit for your date? Do you offer your date one of yours? No! You revel in the flirtiness of a 17-year-old girl and smugly munch.

You know me by now. I stayed. He told me about his job (top salesman in his sector), his house (semi-detached with a garden), his car (Audi something, brand new), his DIY (conservatory, nearly finished). He told me about his last three exes.

I'm afraid that while I was nodding, smiling, saying *yes*, *no* and *really* in all the right places and even leaning across the table in cleavage-enhancing encouragement, my brain was like a Nutribullet, whizzing together the ingredients of revenge.

For our second date, I met Gary at an Italian restaurant. I left work with a chirpy wave. Mrs Patel looked surprised given the chronic constipation I had claimed and the capsules she had dispensed as a remedy.

For the first half hour, Gary showed more interest than before. I attribute this less to innate curiosity and more to being served by a middle-aged waiter instead of a slinky young waitress. He asked the dating basics — work, family, music — and we discovered a mutual dislike of raspberries (if you must know, it's the hairs; creepy). I was on the verge of revoking my intent for revenge, when Gary started talking about golf. I make no apologies to anyone in the audience but if you insist on talking about your clubs, your club (men only), your handicap and the work league you are "dominating," you should be taken to an abattoir and your dead bones used for glue.

It stiffened my resolve. When he excused himself, I slipped a small sachet out of my bag, mixed the contents into his pasta and gave it a quick stir. A dose of the squits would serve him right.

He made no comment on the taste, so the chilli in his sauce must have masked any bitterness. My heart was pounding by this stage. One of those amazing adrenaline surges that you normally only get from zip wires or trying to book *Hamilton* tickets. I insisted on dessert, showing how relaxed I was by flirting with the waiter over my choice. Then coffee, with a liqueur. *Nothing to see here, I'm relaxed and innocent,* my slow savouring of the Limoncello seemed to say. All the while, I was keeping track of the minutes, so that I could witness Gary's fall from grace.

As we left, he asked if I wanted to go for another drink. I shook my head and said that he should have declared his love of golf earlier, as it was a non-negotiable. With perfect timing, I climbed into the nearest cab as Gary clutched his stomach and let out the most trumpeting fart I have ever heard. I watched out of the back window as he squatted in the street, and I knew that the foul-smelling work of the fast-acting laxatives was underway. My revenge was complete.

Or was it?

Two days later, I was in the pharmacy store room with the news on. News that brought a sweat to my palms. "A man in his 30s has died following an allergic reaction to laxatives."

Mrs Patel was relieved it wasn't me who had suffered. "I forgot to warn you, so imagine if you'd had the reaction — I'd be first in line as a suspect! Mind you, it's a rare reaction."

Let's be clear about this; I had not intended to kill poor Gary. I was just using my pharmaceutical connections (yeah, big time gangster, me) to wreak a little revenge — I had intended just one night of the squits, not an eternity of oblivion.

The next few days were fraught. I deleted my profile and all the messages I had sent but knew it wouldn't stop the police tracking me if they were still linked to Gary's account. Every night, I woke four or five times from sweat-soaked nightmares and during the day, I couldn't shake the sensation of being watched. Every time my mobile buzzed, I thought it would be the police. The questions that buzzed inside my brain were exhausting. Did anyone know Gary had been on a date? Did they know he was on Matchymatchy.com? How long would it take them to track 'MissGuided' to me? It seemed that the answers were no, no, and never. I guess taking laxatives isn't a suspicious activity, even when the taker is allergic to them.

I was at home when the call came, making a cheat's supper of beans on toast that I knew I wouldn't be able to eat. A quiet, sad voice said: "Hello, I'm sorry to bother you but my brother died and your number was in his mobile. I'm calling everyone to let them know." I couldn't say anything, so waited for the woman to continue. "It's Gary Middlecombe. Are you a friend of his?"

My breath stopped for a few seconds, my chest constricting and my pulse booming so hard and fast that I was sure she would hear it. When I spoke, my voice sounded to me as if I'd sucked in helium — high and unnatural. "I'm so sorry for your loss," I managed. "No, no I don't really know him." Well, that was true enough. I continued with: "We met once at...at the golf club and he thought we might have a mutual business interest but we only spoke a few times."

"I see. Well, the funeral is a week on Thursday," she offered. "But I expect that your connection is too loose for you to attend."

"I'm terribly sorry but I'm away on business next week. In the States." Where had this ability to fast-track lies come from? "Otherwise, I would have been there." Liar. "Is there a charity to which I can donate? I didn't know Gary but he struck me as someone who would have preferred that to flowers." Actually, I think he would have wanted flowers; those wasteful signals of popularity and affection.

"That's kind," said the sister. "If you look on Facebook, you'll find the link. It's The Golf Foundation, which I'm sure you'll agree is perfect, given his love of the game."

"Right, of course. I'll make sure to get online later."

"Thank you — err, Cherry is it?"

I reacted quickly. "No, it's Cheryl. Gary must have spelt me wrong in his phone. Well, I must go. Sorry again for your loss; he was far too young to die."

My legs were so weak that I sank to the floor and laid my head on the cool tiles. I threw up the cup of tea I'd managed to force down that afternoon but couldn't move to clear it up. Eventually, I forced myself up and as I mopped the pathetically meagre contents of my belly, I realised that I was off the hook. *My brother died* she had said, not *my brother was killed.*

Later that evening, I made a small donation to the Golf Foundation. To give too much would have stunk of guilt. And who am I kidding — I'm not giving to a charity that teaches kids to aspire to become part of an elite group who spoil a walk with holes, balls, clubs and networking. Instead, I donated all of my holiday savings to medical research into bowel cancer.

I should have been relieved. I was safe. But guilt's not a fleeting emotion. Manslaughter's not something you forget — or forgive — no matter how many abattoir jokes you make.

The migraines started a couple of weeks after that. For two or three days in a cluster, my temples were squeezed by a vice and a jagged line blocked half my vision. Mrs Patel was concerned, told me to go to the doctor. But I couldn't face it; what if I blurted everything out?

She put up with it for a few months; she is a lovely, kind-hearted person. But she had no choice but to sack me three months ago. I don't blame her. You're not much good in a retail setting if you're off more days than you're on and when you're in, you're snapping like a teenager with menstrual tension.

At that point, I regretted the donation to bowel cancer research. I wasn't fit to get another job and money was tight enough already.

I stopped seeing my friends, instead staying in, curled up in front of trash TV box sets. A few kept calling, turning up with soup and chocolates, diagnosing depression rather than the sullied conscience of an accidental murderer. I snapped, said I was fine, refused to see the doctor. I was vile to be around but still my family and my oldest friend, Simon, stuck around, putting up with the bad hygiene, permanent pajamas and near catatonic state.

There is no ache like guilt. It is a tumour in the gut, hidden but all-consuming. I woke up every morning with a black twist of sadness cramping my insides.

That's how I ended up determined to say goodbye to the world. Yeah, sorry, that's not so funny. I'm not sure I'm cut out for this stand-up lark.

I ruled out anything that would make my guts burn and spill out (slow, painful) and figured my chances of buying a gun were slim (I don't live in that part of London). Although car accidents only have a seventy-something percent success rate, I decided that was my method. I'm a fast driver and I knew just the place, a long hill with a sharp bend at the bottom. It was notorious for accidents.

My flat was gleaming after the final clean. Sex toys and erotic fiction were binned and the cobwebs banished. On the dining room table were three pieces of paper: a list of utilities and other direct debits; instructions for accessing my will; and the code for working out my online passwords. I had laid out beautifully written letters on proper stationery for everyone I care about. I was ready.

I voted against Dutch courage. Alcohol could lead to tears, which could lead to wavering and a desperate phone call or three. At eight on the dot I set off. I drove carefully, determined not to speed. I kept going for three hours and waited until midnight. I did a test run of the hill, driving cautiously so I could work out where to veer off.

I pulled over and paused because now the tears had started. The guilt and the hurt and the heartache were spilling out and I howled and screamed.

Once I had calmed down, I traced back a mile before the hill, accelerated, powered down and stayed true to my course, hitting 100 miles per hour. I crashed. Crashed through the barrier and tumbled over and over down the hill.

They found me the next morning. I had done it.

Except that I hadn't. I flunked it.

Mine was in the twenty-something percent of crashes that don't end in death. Two months on and I'm still in a persistent vegetative state with no hope of recovery. So much for the wannabe comic at open mic night — but at least this whiles away the night hours when everyone's asleep.

I have to distract myself somehow. Otherwise, my regrets flood in, along with a perverse obsession with food. I torture myself with dreams of rich food — sweet lobster with garlic butter; pasta with a truffle sauce; the roast potatoes and yorkshire pudding from a Sunday roast; my mum's sherry trifle. And oh, I'd kill for a glass of really good red wine. Not literally, although what have I got to lose?

I feel nothing at all physically. So my endless fantasies of food don't make me hungry. I feel no thirst. Sure, there are advantages to this. I have no sense of being turned, swabbed, needles going in and out, no pain. But I can't feel my hand being held, can't move, can't wake up and tell them I'm here. More than anything, I want to be able to feel my eyes open and see the faces of my loved ones.

Yes, it might surprise you to learn that I'm loved. I have no doubt of it now — a little too late in life. A rich theatre of affection, warmth and anguish has played out in front of me. It turns out that Simon has loved me for years but was too shy to tell me. I don't know whether to slap him or kiss him. Both probably; if I could. I've always had a crush on him but assumed he was gay and still in the closet. And now I have his tears rather than kisses, although I can't feel them. But Sandra, my eldest sister, told him he was dripping on me one day. Posey, my younger sister, prayed out loud that I would feel his tears and wake up. Personally, I'd rather Simon sang 'Girlfriend in a Coma' to make me laugh.

I feel so stupid not knowing how loved I was, even when I was curled up in a ball on the sofa. They're all feeling guilty for not seeing how bad things had become — why didn't I do more? is Mum's frequent lament. I should have taken her home and looked after her. I want to tell them all how much I love them, how sorry I am. I want to take each and every person in my arms and make it okay. I want to stop their tears; end their grief, end mine.

My parents know how strongly I feel about switching off the machines and not hanging on with pointless hope. So, they're stepping up, being brave, following my wishes.

And here's me, suddenly desperate to live, trying so hard to think, to be funny, to tell these stories, to perform. I don't know why the machines aren't picking up my brain activity. I like to think of it as Gary's revenge.

After nine weeks, today's the day. They are about to switch off the machines. They've been with the doctors for some time, talking through the plan for the last time. And nothing I can think of triggers a spike on the graph. They're coming in and who knows how long it will take for my thoughts to dissipate and leave me in peace.

So that's all from me. I've been Cherry McFarlane and you've been a great audience. Thank you and goodbye.

THE END

RECIPE FOR DISASTER

Alexander Walker

I turned the keys. I flicked the switches. I let the fluorescents flicker to life as I blinked through the sleep. I shrugged off my coat with a slow roll of both shoulders, pushed off my trainers and pulled out the slippers from under the bench. *The best work is done as comfortably as possible.* I left my keys in a bowl which balanced upon a stone troll vaguely imitating Atlas. My apron hung on the opposite peg, regularly washed but bearing many burn scars from the years. I pulled it over my head and wrapped the tassels tight, pulling them round front and tying a bow that tucked into the front pocket. As I did, a familiar jingle of leftover coins rang from the fabric pouch. The coffee machine beeped its good morning from ignition and soon the sound and smell of bittersweet relief filled the quiet space. The radio scrambled to life in my hands, turned low to add ambience, lyrics robbed of comprehension. On odd occasion coffee dripped in time to the beat. The thermostat clicked and the boiler woke like the shake of a large duvet. The pilot light waved me greeting from its small window in the machine. *Good to see you too, buddy.* I set my notebook on the side, edges of brightly coloured post-its peeking out from their place-holding, and clicked the ovens on one by one. The first two, immediate with their low hiss of the gas, the snap of the spark and the roar of the flame. The last, a long drawn out sigh as the spark failed to take. The clicks chased each other as I continued to press, forcing me to resort to matches. At the end of the burning head the rows of jets burst into bright blue flame one after the other like a bed of flowers blooming in the sunshine.

I dug out a mug from a shelf full of squabbling trolls, as if the fluorescents had caught them mid-argument and turned them to stone. Andrew always moved these shits around.

I poured the coffee, clicked the walkie-talkie on in its holder and pressed the signal button a couple times to let Andrew know I was down below. He double beeped back in response.

"How you doing, fuckface?" he crackled.

"All good below," I replied, "how's that cold treating you?" The walkie made his nasal voice whine more than usual.

"Oh, fuck off," Andrew scoffed, a hint of a smile in his voice.

"That's 'fuck off, over.'" I replied.

He did not.

Content with the trio of waking behemoths I turned my attention to the beaten, boxy trunk kept in one corner. I wheeled it to the sideboard, unlatching the oversized buckles with a small key, and revealed the meticulously packed rows of jars, boxes and utensils inside. After flicking to the marked page in the notebook I picked out the correct ingredients. Mason jars of coloured spices with spring lids weary from use. Metal containers wearing the faded dirtied echoes of all the adhesive labels that had come before. Bags of fabric tied with twine, vacuum sealed plastic, and a velvet drawstring which rattled upon rest. A thick chopping board of such dark wood it looked burned. A granite pestle and mortar, carved to last, and so heavy it was more apt to break the floor first.

I sipped from the mug and ran a finger down the page. Like the rest it was dog-eared from overuse. Black pen now faded and flanked by blue and red, scribbles over scribbles and mad crossings-outs. As my finger passed I mentally ticked off each ingredient. All set.

I hurriedly composed the scene, adjusting a short stone goblin that held the spatulas. I snapped a photo and sent it to Emily. Just another day in the office.

I plucked a pair of plastic gloves from the box. The dusty talcum powder bloomed as each snapped at the wrist. It was time to prepare the meat.

The walk-in cooler was full and I had to inspect several labels before I brought out the one with the right date and let it rest, taking the chill off before baking.

I had everything I needed. I clapped once, turned up the radio then began.

Stalks were chopped into fine rings, the side of the knife pressed against my curled fingers as the blade on board kept time with the tempo.

Sprigs from larger branches were torn and pinched to release the flavours.

Spoonfuls of coloured powders and pastes fell into the wooden bowl and were mixed with gusto.

Salt crystals were ground into fine powders and mixed with a variety of oils giving way to a rainbow luminescence.

A cursory prod of the meat revealed it was ready, the divot slowly sprang back.

From the velvet bag, small pebbles were laid to rest in a vial of red wine.

The errant coins from my pouch plinked in a dish of vodka before they were consumed by blue flame.

I scooped two handfuls of the saltmix, scattered it over the meat, and then began to scrub. Coarse, firm circular motions. Feeling the landscape of flesh and fat, squeezing to the point of unrelenting bone.

I dipped the pastry brush into the spice bowl then ran it over the salted meat with confident, smooth strokes. A pebble from the vial of wine sat where each line intersected.

I swung a thurible over the meat, its chain wrapped around my palm. Once gold but now faded from decades of use, it swung gently with all the precision of a pendulum, allowing the woodsmoke to cascade and the smell to fill the room.

I removed the coins from the dish and inspected them, they were not perfect but would have to do. I placed them with a delicate tap.

Lastly, I removed the needle from the row of utensils, held it to the end of my thumb and pierced the glove and skin with it as I had a hundred times before. It stung but the sensation was familiar. I withdrew it slowly and let the single bead of blood drip over the centre. My thumb tucked into my palm and red smeared inside the glove.

From above came a slight sound of car doors opening and closing followed by echoes of several pairs of feet slowly shuffling above. The light in the corner of the room turned orange. Andrew was ready.

I regarded my work, suitably content.

This meat was male, almost six foot and older than usual. The salt crystals caught the light, giving the pale skin a diamond quality. The face rested in an eternal sleep decorated by the dark lines of the paste. The coins, sterilised and silver, lay over the eyes and one under the tongue. His hands lay at his sides in peace. I gave the naked man a final look of concern and fetched the coffin lid, sealing him inside his mahogany tomb. I ticked a couple boxes on the clipboard and wheeled the trolley to the elevator. The coffin slid into the grooves and a button press took it up to be witnessed. The light went out.

The familiar drone of the church organ CD that played through speakers behind a faux-organ construction seeped through the ceiling. I had a good twenty minutes so I snapped off the gloves, flicking them to the bin, and gave my thumb a cursory suck. I grabbed the clipboard from the now-vacant trolley and headed out the fire escape for a cigarette, propping the door with one of the many broken stone trolls from the alleyway. As I drew in smoke, distracted by the odd booming syllable of the lectern mic, I looked over the paperwork.

Mr. Baycroft had been seventy-three, a retired electrical engineer, a father of three, a grandfather of five, and had suffered from an aneurysm while gardening. For all of his successes and fortunes his entire life had been reduced to a couple of ticked or unticked boxes on a single sheet of paper. As for his body, that had lain in a wooden box adorned with glyphs and offerings to end its journey in the belly of an industrial oven. To be traded along with all the others that came before it, his flesh, muscle and bone given to something on the other side. Except, the instructions were not always clear, quantities not always exact. We had been through countless trials and errors and I thought we would be in store for a lot more before we got exactly what we wanted. *After all, practice does make perfect.*

My phone pinged. *Bring me back something sweet*, Emily had replied.

I heard the same outro track I'd heard a thousand times

before, flicked the burnt-out butt to the ground and kicked the stone troll from the door letting it shut behind me. The corner light clicked green as Andrew initiated the lift, returning the dark wood box to me, and to its inevitable end. I took another glance at the open notebook, unlatched the trolley and wheeled it to the oven. The heavy metal door slammed shut behind it and I rolled the temperature dials to full.

I clicked the walkie signal a couple times and the light went out.

"Want anything from the shop?" crackled Andrew.

"Nah, all good," I said, not wanting him to disturb me.

The notebook lay open on a different ritual, illustrations decorated the page in red and blue biro, each from a different hand. The book was vast. Sheets stapled to sheets, some faded and taped, collected over decades, maybe even centuries, to finally end up in our hands. It included a plethora of rituals, some simple, some complex, like some cruel cookbook that we had added our own notes to where we had made substitutions.

For this ritual, a new set of ingredients sat on the bench. A corpse lay in its wooden box with each hand folded over the chest, a driven stake held them all together. I used a calligraphy brush to stain the skin with the correct ash paints the notebook described. I had a scalpel in one hand and small crystals in the other, slowly pushing them under the skin into the natural ley lines of the human body, when the door was thrust open.

"I know you didn't want anything but it's such a nice day I thought you'd—", Andrew said from the opening door. "What the bloody fuck do you think you're doing?" he followed, low and slow, as his eyes narrowed, his skin paled, and he dropped the ice cream with a wet smack.

I stared up at him, frozen, glasses slipping from my nose,

sleeves rolled to the elbow. The blade of the scalpel caught the light as it hung above the flesh. He looked sick.

"It's — uh — it's not what it looks like," I said meekly.

His hands shook."Wh—What have you done to her?"

He made his way over to the open casket.

"This —" he started.

"Mmm," I winced,

"This — ugh." His face was disgusted.

"Look, it's —" but he shut me up with a stare.

"This is wrong!" he whispered. "You can't...you're not supposed to...to...to use these crystals like that!" he said, swiping them from my hand."These...these were fucking expensive!" He was out of breath, but persisted nonetheless. "Remember what we talked about?"

"Oh, I remember. You fix the numbers, I fix the meat."

"Meat? Right, I forgot you were still calling them that."

"Yeah, well you don't have to put your hands in them everyday." I replied.

"Still. This isn't in the recipe," he said.

I rolled my eyes. "*Recipe* is more of a food thing and this..." gesturing to the decorated and desecrated corpse before us "...is anything but food-related."

"Whatever. What even is *this*?" He pinched the gem to the light like a diamond inspector.

"It's meteorite from South America. It negates the need for—"

"All I know is I paid for it, and the book doesn't say to use it like *this*." Andrew forced the stone back into my hand as he shook his head. "Next time follow the *recipe*, got it?"

I shrugged. "Like that's made much difference so far."

His eyebrows rose, but before he could utter a sardonic riposte the oven timer beeped.

"Baycroft?"

I nodded and moved to the oven.

With a hand on the handle I looked at him, he was nervous too.

"Well go on then, we haven't got all bloody day."

I opened the large metal door. Dry heat washed out as the smell of soot and ash filled the room. I began to roll the tray out.

"Slow...slowly," Andrew said, hovering.

"Will you just let me fucking do it."

He stepped back.

The tray was empty save for a small mound of ash and scraps in the centre. It was arranged in a perfect pyramid. The octogram we had etched on the tray glowed green like the gas jets on low. Lines from the points cut through the middle of the pile and gave the oven a sickly hue. The pebbles placed on Mr. Baycroft remained but had lost their marble edge and were now completely black. They sat inside the eight triangles of the octagram.

"I thought they were meant to end up at the corners?" Andrew remarked.

They were. Or at least, that's where the correct sprite was meant to leave them.

"Maybe this is something else?" he said again, filling the silence.

He leant his hand towards them but jerked it back when the pyramid shifted.

"I didn't...it wasn't m—"

"Shhhut the fuck up," I hissed.

The pyramid shook again, small waves of ash crumbling in a miniature avalanche. We stared as the pyramid shook several more times to reveal an egg that lay at the centre. It rocked back and forth at regular intervals as whatever lay inside tossed and turned.

"It's an egg," Andrew said.

"Your powers of observation are astounding," I whispered, as I reached for it.

"Whoawhoawhoa—" but my glance quieted him.

"It might be hot is all," he whispered with a shrug.

I scooped the egg from the remains of the ashen pyramid. It was, in fact, freezing cold. I blew the remains of Mr. Baycroft from the shell and Andrew coughed overdramatically.

The egg rocked in my hands. Like a cannonball amidst stormy seas, it was heavy and constantly avoiding restraint. It was green and blue and the shell seemed to shift like oil on water, swirling like storm clouds or a rolling surf. A tap broke the silence. Andrew's eyes met mine immediately. A second followed shortly after, punctuating the silence that surrounded us. As the shell cracked the swirling reacted around it, as if the cracks were lightning in a storm.

I felt the heavy ball move against me and had to steady my hands for fear of dropping it. We had received eggs before, of many different sizes and colours and all with slightly different inhabitants. The pentagoblin had wrought its own special kind of hell over one bank holiday weekend, forcing us to replaster most of the walls. The pygmy serpent had, likewise, caused a proper mess and chewed on a couple of corpses before we managed to wrangle it into shackles. Both had fetched a high price on the market, enough for the meteorite crystals that currently lay half in and out of Mrs. Hewitt.

A fracture of shell flew loose and a torrent of sulphurous slime spilled out over my hands. I turned and handled the opening egg with a careful grip. More pieces broke and fell as the thing inside thrashed with increased frequency. Vague shapes of limbs could be made out through the thick slime and embryonic sac as the thing stretched and tore at its bindings.

In a sudden crackle of shell the thing inside shook itself free.

I sighed. "It's another fucking troll."

"Fuck's sake," Andrew hissed and immediately lost interest.

The troll sat in my open hands, both stumpy legs stuck out from its drooping belly and one stubby finger stuck up its nose. Snot and bile seemed to leak from its very skin.

"Here, you take—" I gestured at Andrew.

"I'm not fucking taking it, I don't have gloves on."

"Always leaving me to do the dirty work," I said, shaking my head,

"Here. Dump it in this." He held up a bucket.

I chucked the slimy, eggy mess into the bucket and dropped it into the sink as the troll protested.

"Say a few words?" I said but before Andrew could open his mouth I turned the tap on. He winced as the thing shrieked and thrashed for a few seconds then all became quiet.

"Here," I said, handing him the dripping stone corpse from the bucket. "Do some of the dirty work for a change and put this with the rest on your way out. I've got to get Mrs. Hewitt ready for tomorrow."

Andrew took it meekly and shuffled towards the door.

"Maybe it's just the recipe."

"Oh fuck off, Andrew. And clean up that ice cream on your way out."

He did not.

I left Mrs. Hewitt resting, prepared and ready for the next day. She could wait. Enjoy another night's rest before the burn. The lights flickered out and ceased their fluorescent fizz. The keys clicked and the doors locked. I shuffled round to the front of the building, idling with my phone in hand.

I text Emily. *No luck.*

She responded barely a minute later. *Sad face.*

My foot glanced a stone troll on the ground and it toppled into a group of others. The arrangement of grotesques at the entrance was often admired by mourners, some even snapped photos for themselves despite the sombre occasion. Stumpy stone trolls sat at the front, fat stone bellies hanging over fat stone knees. Thinner, taller goblins stood or crouched behind, long fingers covering their faces as they had cowered from the water. At least these ones had been complete. Although they were the sum of our failures — nobody would pay for a troll or a goblin — the screaming half-torsos and creeping severed hands had been worse.

Emily messaged again. *Always next time.*

"Always next time," I whispered, to no-one but the trolls.

THE END

ROOK'S MOVE

Sam Derby

It was an Azore wind: he could taste it. It had brought the desert here to this green land, the red Saharan sun of his dreams, riding in the English sky. It was the month of October, in the year of their lord 1654. It was the month of Heshwan, in the year of his lord 5415. It was warm, unseasonably so, even now in the late afternoon. It was an Azore wind.

"This wind," yelled Cirques, the old fool, from across the street, "is from the Wadi Rum. I have a book — back in Damascus," — he always had a book back in Damascus — "that maps the winds! Can you imagine it? The great learning that I left behind."

"A shame you didn't bring more of it with you!" Jacob shot back.

"Hah! You disagree then?"

Jacob paused. "I can taste the Sahara," he said, "and the red sun..."

"Atmospheric dust, fifty miles up, or so says Ibn Mu'adh," shouted Cirques, "so I can't tell you which desert it comes from. But it reminds us of home, yes?"

Jacob nodded reluctantly, toying with a pawn, eyeing the latent rook at one edge of the board. They played chess, each with his own set, across Oxford's broad High Street. Each sat beside the door of his own coffee house, at a low table brought far from home, calling out moves to each other over the clatter of hooves and boots and coach-wheels. They sat there despite the rain and the snow and the cold, like they had done in a warmer country. They drank coffee. Customers came and went, talking and laughing and arguing. Some crossed the road to move from one coffee house to the other, some moved on to the taverns that surrounded them.

"You listen to too many folk tales, Jacob," said Cirques, a little later. "What's wrong with the natural philosophy of our forefathers? We brought more to these shores than coffee, you know."

"As you tell me each time we play."

Jacob looked back at the chess board in front of him. Even after so many games, his vision was clouded beyond one or two moves. Something about that rook was disturbing him. The word triggered something. Mr Rukh. Ten years ago, it must have been.

This bone-rattling, nose-blistering, hair-coarsening, mind-boggling road. Why, when he had looked out across the rooftops of his home town of Safed, in Galilee, at the pulsing sandstorm racing not out of the Syrian desert, but inland, from across the sea, had he still wanted to leave? The camels were loaded, the camel-pullers had been paid and were liable to drink. A single move had set some mysterious series of events into motion, and he did not know how to stop it. So a few hours later they were in the middle of the storm, stinging skin and blasted eyes beneath that strange red sun. And all around them, the hot brass smell of the Sahara. That's what the camel-pullers said anyway. Jacob was in the midst of the caravan, protected to some extent by those on either side of him. But the sand had still invaded everything: clothes, body and mind. After the first week, when the agony of camel riding had subsided to a throb at the top of each thigh, the sand monopolised his thoughts. Scraping away at him, thinning him out somehow. They were bound from Safed to Acre on the Galilean coast, carrying their precious cargo. Under the guidance of Mr Rukh.

"Hey, friend — Jacob — it's your move!"

"I was back in Galilee."

"You should have visited that coffee house I told you about, in Acre. Your own might be more successful! Hah!"

Jacob ignored him. The two coffee-houses of Oxford, on either side of the curved and cobbled High Street, made better companions than they did rivals. Plenty of passing trade from the coaches that drew up outside the Angel, plenty of scholars seeking the stimulation of coffee for their debates and conjurations.

And once the novelty of having a coffee house in Oxford at all had worn off, the arrival of Cirques' rival operation had done much to rejuvenate trade for Jacob. Now there was a firm set of loyal customers of each, plus a sizeable group who enjoyed the movement between the two, and the excuse it gave to start new conversations, and to end the ones that were headed up blind allies.

"I owe my meagre success to you, my friend, I know," Jacob replied drily, dropping the pawn and moving his knight out of danger instead.

"And I learnt everything from you, master," the old fool shouted back, gesturing rudely, but half-smiling as he did so in the fading sun. "You know, you made your first bad move back in Galilee. You should have landed at Famagusta. I could have shown you. I have this book, back in Damascus, of all the trade routes, of all the caravans. All the times, the tides, the pirates — everything. The Mediterranean is a very gentle sea. Acre, Famagusta, and then Venice. Fast, safe, the modern way to travel."

"You know that I wanted to follow the pilgrim road, to visit Byzantium," Jacob replied, as he always did, "to see the great ruins, the temples, Hagia Sophia. It was so beautiful."

"Byzantium — you old romantic. *Istanbul* it has been for I don't know how many years. Centuries, no? And you told me you hated that journey. You hated the road, and the sand, and the camels. Especially the camels."

"I loved the sunsets."

"The sun? The sun is for telling the time."

Mr Rukh had taken them on a square-rigged galleon across the Bay of Haifa, to Famagusta. The sea had raced past Jacob as he sat in thought. Fortress-topped cliffs in the distance drifted more slowly. Beneath each fortress there would once have been a temple, crushed to its foundations. There was only a dim remembrance of each temple now, among the elders of each island, in the ballads of each village. Soon there would be none, except in local dialects: in the word for the way that the cliff rose from the sea, or for describing how the sun draped shadows on an olive grove; words that conjured unexpected gods. The town of Famagusta sprang down from the hillside to the harbour. As if although built high for safety and for the protection of its children, it had yearned for the touch of the sea. Jacob blinked and focused on the nearer shoreline. There were Ottoman vessels so close you could count the teeth of each captain. There was something wrong. What was that story he had been told back in Acre? About the 'Sea People' who lurked in dark ships around the coast of Cyprus, taking their pick from the merchant ships who docked too far east, too far west, or in the hours of the night when the harbour guards were heavy with drink. They would take his cargo, and take him hostage. He remembered what happened to the hostages in that story.

Cirques had crossed the road and stood over Jacob's board, studying the position, looking back to his own place from time to time. He picked up a bishop, after a little while, and toyed with it for a few seconds, before looking Jacob in the eye, and advancing it with some emphasis.

"Fortune favours the brave," he said.

"It wasn't sentimentality that drove me to Byzantium, you know," said Jacob, after looking for a move for some minutes, "It was cowardice. I made a deliberate decision not to dock, and to go by land. Against the advice of my guide. It saved my life, I think."

"You worry too much. You moved west too slowly in any case. While I was in Venice making money, you were wasting time."

"You were not a free man, in Venice, though, like I was in Byzantium, were you? You were locked in behind the great gates of the ghetto every night, not so?"

"I was a rich man."

"Then we were both happy."

"We might have shared coffee in Famagusta if you had followed the advice of your guide, and docked," said Cirques, beneath his breath, not giving it up.

It was almost evening now, but the way that the slant golden light still lit the stone made the city glow as if it were yet noon.

"You were in Famagusta? You never told me this," Jacob said.

"Just for a few weeks. We sailed, like you, out of Acre, and docked there to take on water and food, and to enjoy ourselves a little."

"It's one of those towns."

Cirques grunted, smiling. "There was a coffee house — run by a man expelled from Valencia a few years earlier. We talked, about Venice, about the life there — for Jews, I mean. He said that the taxes were heavy and the people were friendly. Two sides of the same coin. And there was none of that — other stuff. With the yellow stars, you know. And no Inquisition sniffing around."

Jacob was silent for a moment; he moved a pawn forward on the king's side. "I heard those stories. Did he not mention the ghettoes?"

"Ghettoes, yes, he mentioned the ghettoes. But a man could do business in those ghettoes. With almost everyone, outside the walls or inside."

"Almost everyone?"

"There are always bad apples," said Cirques, waving a hand. "Tell me Jacob: did you visit the ghetto in your *Byzantium*?"

The unmistakable jangle and clatter of a familiar tongue — a drier, sandblasted language — filled the streets as sundown approached. The Jews had made this place their own, walled off from the rest of the town. And the apartness of language made that wall higher and thicker. A language that knew the value of names, and their power. That held locked within its nature and structure the very name of God. Jacob made his slow way down through the street. Here in the shops and inns of the Sakyra Caddesi there was no feeling of cabala, or mysticism, like there was in his home town of Safed, where the mystics and the ascetics seemed to cluster like bees around bulls-tongue. The dark closed in as he sat down at the furthest table from the door, watching children dance in the dusty street. There was a bustle in the agora that spoke not of great riches, at this moment, but great industry. There was a feeling of desperate purpose about the narrow streets crammed with stalls and the tables similarly crammed with goods. Not just because of the Ottomans, tales of whose bloody exploits circulated as freely as coins bearing a Frankish stamp, but from some momentum borne there by the movement of those people from across the sea. In the tavern, though, there was stillness: people came and went; old men came and stayed. An hour later and Jacob still sat waiting, a steaming glass of strong sweet tea between his fore-fingers and thumb. With those delicate fingers he greeted diplomats; with his leathery thumb, bitten into by blades, he greeted merchants. The deep red liquid in the samovar in the centre of the room glowed softly, like the blood of the city, like the blood of the East.

"Look at you, you're back there now," said Cirques, "you feel too much, my friend. That's why you let those *Marranos* rip you off every time."

"Why do you call them that? *Marranos*?"

"That — that's just what they call them in Venice. Us, I mean. The Jews."

"It means pig, doesn't it?"

"So it does, so it does," said Cirques, looking up at him, "but you know, I had forgotten that. The word had lost something for me. In repetition, first, and then perhaps in time. There are so many people there, so many words, Jacob: Venice is the meeting place of the world! A great place for a coffee house! Which is why you should have come there, too." Cirques moved his Queen's Bishop's pawn forward, then sat lost in thought.

Cirques fumbled with his portable sundial, trying to get the incline set right for this part of the world — for an island off the Dalmatian coast in the southern Adriatic en route to Venice. He was not concerned about setting up in business, not in the Veneto. Certainly, in places like this, on the uncivilised *outskirts of the Empire, there might be the occasional problem — with his Jewishness. But not in Venice. Hadn't his cousin sent so much gold back to Damascus, after all?*

"Marrano," cried a voice, coming from out of the sun's glare to the port side of the xebec. Cirques looked out into the dark beneath the glare, his hand striving to block out the sun.

"Marrano, have you paid your taxes yet? I am the tax collector here, Marrano."

The voice was more insistent than it was threatening; certainly, there would be some kind of harbour tax. And a landing tax. And a disembarkation tax. Not to mention a high price at any tavern he might be able to find which could provide something that he could just about believe might be kosher. But it would be different in Venice: elegant meetings with merchant princes, over elegant meals, with the scent of coffee saturating the air. His cousin had written of the wise counsel available for Jewish merchants, from a consigliere *who could help him.*

"Now you're dreaming, Cirques my friend," said Jacob, "but it can't have been so wonderful, or why would you have left for Amsterdam?"

Cirques looked up at him, his eyes narrowing. "I was lucky.

I was helped in Venice, just as my cousin had told me I would be. A great merchant took me under his wing, became my *consigliere*. His advice made me rich, so that I could leave when the trouble started. That's all it was. You can tell yourself otherwise, friend. I left Venice because I wanted to. Now tell me, why did you leave Istanbul?"

"It was a time of great change," said Jacob, with deep irony, remembering the great rebellion: the rumble of gunfire in the distance and the flash of swords. The locking of the palace gates, and the screams of men and horses coming from behind them.

"Times of great change can be good for business."

"But bad for those of us trading from the side-streets, rather than from the centre of the *agora*," said Jacob, nudging forward another pawn.

Cirques nodded and sipped his coffee. The High Street was quiet for a moment — the last coach had gone, and the students were under curfew; it was not yet dark enough to hide the escape of those who could bribe the gatekeeper or scale the wall. The sun dipped behind the tower of St Mary's, and Jacob sat in its shadow, and shivered.

"There was a caravan leaving for Vienna, a week after the murder of the infant Sultan, taking the usual things — spices, jewellery, all fine stuff. I left nothing behind. As I made my gradual way north-west, through the Lutheran states, the walls around the ghettoes grew smaller. There were still yellow stars and circles, and places where we were more welcome than others, but the walls grew smaller until, in Amsterdam, there was no ghetto at all, and they disappeared. I still wonder if I saw you there, Cirques."

"This place reminds me of the ghetto," said Cirques, looking across the board at Jacob, a coffee cup in his hands. The steam rose from the cup and around his face, encircling the sparse dark curls around his temples. He picked up the exposed bishop without enthusiasm, moving it back to its starting point

"Oxford?"

"Yes. The high stone walls, and the heavy gates."

"I thought the walls of the ghetto didn't stop you doing business."

"No, no, not at the start." Cirques paused. "It changed though, it did change. It was — there was something more serious about the locking of the gates, each night, after a while; like the tales my Valencian friend had told me, of the constant Inquisitions which drove him east to Venice. And when they locked the gates: the dreadful sound of it all. I could hear them on the other side, whispering "*Marrano, marrano,*" through the lock to us. I would wake in the night and hear odd words and soft cries. They rounded us up each night, all of us with our yellow hats on."

"And so?"

"And so I stopped wearing the yellow hat. Started wearing a crucifix. A man has to do business."

"But a man's soul, Cirques? A man's soul cannot be disguised."

"What is a soul, Jacob? Where do you find it? I have a book..."

"Back in Damascus?"

"Back in Damascus: a book of mortuary skills, of mummification. Let me tell you, you can empty out a body entirely of stuff, pull it out with your hands and scour the insides, and still not find a soul that you could extract and bottle up. There is no soul that you can hold in your fist. You talk of souls..."

"Peace, my friend, peace, I meant no disrespect..."

"You talk of souls. I talk of business. So I wore the damned crucifix. Much good it did me."

"Aha!" said Jacob, after a while, advancing his rook and

looking up at Cirques.

"Is that checkmate? No, not yet," said Cirques, half to himself, and then to Jacob, "It was profitable to be a Christian, for a while. My *consigliere* helped me to trade, unnoticed. He told me about you, perhaps."

"About me? You never said this before."

"I never realised until now. He said, there's a Jew I knew in Istanbul..."

"Byzantium," put in Jacob, with a smile.

"In Istanbul," repeated Cirques, pursing his lips to repress a laugh, "who wants to take coffee to Amsterdam. I told him no-one would be such a fool."

"So that's how you stole my idea?"

"I will not stoop to answer your accusation, my friend," said Cirques wryly, "Let's say I knew that you would appreciate some company. But Amsterdam was — well, you must have found the same."

"Full of Jewish coffee houses."

"Exactly. We thought we were in the vanguard, but everyone else had fled before we did, when the war began."

"And so to England."

"And so to England. And then why did you come here, to Oxford?"

"I followed the river," said Jacob.

"You are such a romantic. I followed the scholars. Philosophers, astronomers, mathematicians. Anyone who had time to sit, and think, and talk."

"And drink coffee."

They raised their cups in unison and drank.

"We should take our game to a tavern, now the sun has gone down," said Cirques, moving another pawn, "and drink to those who have helped us. I give you the *consigliere:* Signor Rocca, Signor Rook."

"Yes, a tavern," said Jacob, making a mental note of the position, before standing to leave; and then he turned sharply to look at Cirques. "Did you call him, Signor Rook?"

Cirques had the same dream, again and again: he was washed ashore in Venice. A little wooden boat in which he slept drifted past the columns of San Marco, and then along the centre of the Grand Canal, drawn in a spiral into Venice. Waves pushed and slapped it around churlishly, mews mocked the passing of the sun. The darkness was absolute, save for the lights on the buildings on the canal-side, like a pin-pricked cloth hung across the sun. Three men, two dark-skinned like him and one paler, all wearing black hats, awaited him in the centre of the city. They stared as he climbed from the boat into the centre of a vast and palatial square.

"Here is your yellow hat," said the first man, in a thick Germanic accent.

"Here is your red hat," said the second, in a voice he recognised from the islands. ("Marrano," he heard once more.)

"Here is your black hat," said the third, in a voice from his own birthplace.

Cirques reached out his hand and took the black hat. Two of the three men nodded, and turned away as one, walking off into the shadow that was one with the dark water of the canal. The third man raised his arm and pointed a long finger at Cirques. Cirques tried to hide, to pull the man's arm down, to avoid that gaze somehow, but the sun came relentlessly up and he could not escape. The people of Venice crowded the towers of the city and looked down upon him. He covered his face in his hands. And then he woke.

"I think it may have been Signor Rook — Signor Rocca — who betrayed me," said Cirques after a little while, sitting with Jacob in the Saracen's Head. They drank ale that was as dark as their coffee. The game was before them once more.

"Betrayed you? Your *consigliere*?"

"In a cafe, in Venice, outside the ghetto. I was not wearing my yellow hat; I was talking to a fellow Jew, a man from Safed, actually. It was a business meeting, with my cousin, the usual things. I thought I saw Signor Rocca through the doorway; I even raised my hand to wave, but he seemed not to see me. And then there were six or seven of them around me."

"I never knew you were betrayed. You said that you left because you wanted to."

"Betrayal is something we all risk to some extent, not so? I had to pay — a court official here, a churchman there, bodyguards. But I could pay. At least I could pay. And so I could leave with my head held high. Of my own free will. My cousin was less lucky."

"What happened to him?"

"He was prosecuted, fined a fortune."

"I'm sorry for it," said Jacob, poring over the board.

"Don't be, he made one again. No keeping that one down. What about you?"

"Me? I was never prosecuted. Beaten, once. I don't know why."

"In golden Byzantium?"

"Yes, even there. They changed the rules. There was a notice on the town hall gate. A new curfew, new taxes." Jacob took a bishop with his pawn, opening up a whole rank to the King's rook.

"A trap. Hah." Cirques ignored the pawn, and moved his knight instead.

"Sometimes I think that I also was betrayed," said Jacob.

"You, betrayed?"

"By Master Rukh. My guide, who almost delivered me to the Turkish wolves, in Famagusta."

"You believe it was deliberate?"

"He was so insistent: this must be the harbour, this must be the night...and those dark ships circling us, and the hills lined with houses that looked like tombstones...I had a bad feeling..."

"You and your feelings."

"Perhaps my feelings kept me from trouble, for a little while," said Jacob.

"Perhaps Master Rukh was an honest man, and all you did was lose time."

"Master Rukh. This is the kind of move he would have made, the devil," said Jacob, sliding forward a rook and looking up at Cirques with a glint in his eye.

"A bold strike," said Cirques, "from the soul, though, rather than the rational mind. Why do they call it a 'rook' here, anyway? It looks more like a *tzariach,* like a tower." He paused for a little while, as something struck him. "The word for the tower is *rocca* in Venice. Isn't that strange?"

"It is?" said Jacob, impatiently looking at the board where his trap lay ready to be sprung.

"Master Rukh. Signor Rocca, who told me about a Jew he knew in Istanbul."

"Who made his fortune preying on Jewish merchants," said Jacob, "do you think...?"

"It was the same man. The same devil," said Cirques, thumping the table dramatically so that the pewter tankards leapt and clanked against the oak table, spilling precious ale in the process, "whose evil clutches we both escaped!"

"Then I *was* betrayed," said Jacob, solemnly. And then broke out into a smile. "You know..."

"When we talk like this, you mean? Are you suggesting that..."

"We can get caught up a little in the story, Cirques my friend. We can elaborate, rather."

"Where was he from, though, do you think, this great devil?" said Cirques, not wanting to leave the story unresolved, his hand hovering over the board.

"He was an Arab, a Persian Arab. He told me that *rukh* meant "war chariot". And now that I think of it, that's the name of the piece, in Persia, is it not?"

"That is very satisfying to know, Jacob my friend. And if you ask the barmaid in this tavern, she will tell you that a rook is a swindler. Now: having remembered or created Mr Rook, we should thank him, should we not, if he was indeed our betrayer?"

Jacob looked up at him. "Thank him?"

"For bringing us here. For bringing us together," said Cirques.

Jacob's eyes darkened for a moment, and then he looked up at his friend, and smiled a very open smile.

Cirques smiled too, a different kind of smile, as he picked up his rook, and moved it to the eighth rank. "Checkmate, my friend," he said.

THE END

STASIS

Adam Fields

Two passengers collided. A latte clashed with a panini; the lettuce leaves and slices of foam-skimmed tomato skidded across the departures lounge. Two men in their mid-fifties argued.

"Calm yer horses," said Sally, waving dismissively, "It's just a coffee and a sandwich, theer are people starvin' to death for God's sake, and all you two care about are stains on yer suits! Get over yer sens."

Flabbergasted, with jaws agape, they shared a look and disappeared, leaving Sally to clean up; soon satisfied, she wrung out her mop in Bucket number twelve, and continued her shift on the second floor of the departures lounge of spaceport Barnsley One.

"Come here Bucket Twelve!" she hissed, as it lazily weaved between passengers heading towards the boarding gate.

"Sorry sir, madam, mind of its bloody own!"

"You don't find this kind of chaos at Heathrow One!" spat a woman in a green suit, tapping her watch. The bucket swayed into her path, mirroring her attempts to move past; when finally she broke free and rounded the corner, Sally raised two fingers in her direction.

"Miserable sod."

She snorted, put her earphones in, and hummed along with one of her grandfather's favourite Dizzy Gillespie numbers:

> *If I never have a cent,*
> *I'll be rich as Rockefeller,*
> *Gold dust at my feet,*
> *On the sunny side of the street.*

Underneath a dome of intelligent glass, with ribbons of spiralling adverts, she made her way to make a black coffee on the top floor of the departures lounge: three overlapping tiers of bars, restaurants and boutiques, each lined with cherry blossoms, and yews, and oaks, all caught in permanent autumns and springs. Leaning over the third tier barrier, empty mug in hand, Sally liked to marvel at the impossibility of Barnsley One: within two generations of Apollo 11, humanity had established themselves on Ceres.

Refreshed by the caffeine boost, Sally mopped in large arcs, propelled by her large, powerful forearms.

"Sorry, love, can yer move yer legs, just got to get under there."

Sally couldn't help but linger over the sight of the passenger's unusual clothing. *E.F.O- C. Andrews* read the embroidery on the Temex Corporation jacket, each arm lined with the three jagged, golden strips of a First Officer Engineer, but without the red rimmed blouse, or black and white star patterned shirt; instead, she sported a pair of worn jeans and a tank top.

"Can I help you with something?" said First Officer Andrews, brushing her bitten fingernails through a tangle of black hair as she slouched in the seat.

"I said, can you move your legs, love, I don't ask for much."

First Officer Andrews stayed put. Frustrated, Sally folded

her lips over her teeth, ran her tongue over the cracks, and shook her head whilst she cleaned around the human island, keeping her gaze fixed on the sighing engineer. Nowadays, it was a running theme of passengers in the spaceport to be underwhelmed by their surroundings. Twenty, thirty years ago, the first civilians flew from Barnsley One bound for Ceres; Sally remembered as a child watching the interviews of the humans bound for the stars, and how their eyes bulged with childlike fervour — how easily we become accustomed to the impossible. Now, the only people that smiled here were those with a drink in their hand.

"You oreyt there, love?" said Sally, using the mop as a crutch to lower herself onto the bench.

"Do I look alright?"

"Well, if I'm honest, you look more miserable than most people I see here, if that counts for owt."

"I'd rather you weren't honest," she said, hunching forwards. "Why d'you care anyway?"

"I don't have a chipboard lodged in me head for a start — and it's called tekin' an interest, somethin' we do in these parts."

When Clarke didn't reply, Sally sighed and stood to finish her work.

"Well, can't say I dint try."

The floor shook as she made her way across the third tier of the departures lounge, as it did every day at noon, so Sally turned her headphones up. In the distance, a lone grey column rumbled with clouds at its base: a greatship. Sweeping across the endless tarmac, a smoking monster charged towards her and engulfed the dome in darkness; specs of industrial detritus rained against the glass, and overhead, a blue light could be made out for several moments, propelling passengers on their ten day trip towards the asteroid belt and Ceres. As the natural light peeked through the cracks in the overcast skies, an Assistant unplugged itself from the dock and rolled towards her.

"Miss Sally, there is a passenger still here, a Clarke Andrews, First Order Engineering for the Temex Corporation, departures lounge, on tier three. Would you like me to call security?"

Sally took out her earphones. She assumed it impossible to miss a flight aboard a greatship: not only did a ticket cost twice as much as her home, but the spaceport was managed in such a way that only the passengers bound on the next flight would be allowed into the departures lounge.

"I'll see to it, Assistant," said Sally.

"Then, we will escort you to the threat."

Several black eyes phased into existence as the dozen Assistants left their charging docks and surrounded her, teetering for a command.

"Bloody machines, she's not a threat, she's just havin' a hard time is all. Plain ter see."

"But protocol dictates that..." began another.

"Stuff yer bloody protocol," she said. "I'll sort it."

"Don't mind 'em, madam," said Sally, gesturing to the crowd of Assistants poking around the corner. She clapped twice and the robots dispersed. "Look, love, you shunt be in here. They want to call security, but they won't do owt until I say so. I've been putting the fear of God into 'em for seventeen years, must have taken a hint — don't know how people used to be scared of 'em."

Sally bent down so she was face to face with Clarke. "I know you reyt don't feel like talkin' to me, but you're gonna' have to explain how-"

Clarke sighed, took out her purse, and produced a security pass of a woman with a faded pink bob cut. Sally had to do a double take to check it was her, before pressing the credentials against a thin graphene tablet she produced from her utility belt.

"Miss Sally, how is the threat level?" said an Assistant over her shoulder. Sally leapt back and dropped the tablet on the floor.

"Bloody things gotta' stop creepin' up, yer gunna' kill me — what is it now?" she said bending down, picking up the tablet and waving it in the Assistant's face. "Look! It's flashed green, see here, she's allowed to be here, she's got clearance from the exec!"

The Assistant's two black, digital eyes blinked once, and it rolled away to converse with the others. Checking her wristwatch, Sally was due a short break, so she called for Bucket Twelve, taking out her lunchbox from its storage compartment. She took a seat beside Clarke, who inched away, a few more feet than necessary.

"Me grandad was a miner round here; a job for life, hard graft like, but, it gave him a good standin' in the community, though the pay weren't nowt to shout about. You wunt have thought it, but where weer sittin' now used to be a meadow, with hundreds of miners riding their bikes to an' from the colliery," Sally said. "I wonder about what he'd mek of all this. 'Tekin a ship to a space rock to mine? Some reyt tripe you've got theer lass. Got perfectly good mines down here!'. He was the sorta' man that coulda' designed greatships."

"Look, I don't need this right now, I just want to be by myself..." began a frustrated Clarke.

"Passed 'is eleven plus, 'top of me class', he used to boast," continued Sally unfazed. "He could've walked into Oxford, me mum reckoned."

"I'm sorry, but why are you telling me this?" said Clarke, finally getting a chance to speak.

"Well, I'm just being friendly, love," said Sally, taken aback. "Dint mean owt by it."

"Look," said an exhausted Clarke, looking at the Barnsley One security pass Sally wore around her neck, "Sally, I've just handed my resignation in to a prestigious, directorial role at Temex, where I've worked for since I finished my Masters, a company I was certain I'd spend the rest of my career at...and yet, here I find myself, on a bench, in one of the...the backwater spaceports. I've got a lot on my mind, please can you just..."

"Me daughter is studying for a Masters at the minute, funnily enough," added Sally, cracking open her lunchbox. "She gets her brains from grandad, her dad certainly hasn't got owt goin' on upstairs...and nowt downstairs either," she said, pausing for Clarke's laughter, though when it didn't come, she continued. "But we're reyt proud of her —she's studyin' Astrophysics and Materials Science at The Ceres Chinese University — came top of her college and all!"

"Balliol?" said Clarke meeting Sally's eyes with interest.

"No, Barnsley."

Clearly impressed, Clarke frowned with approval.

"You said your daughter is studying at Ceres University?"

"Aye."

"It's a funny place isn't it? Marvellous, of course, but undoubtedly-"

Sally stifled a snort.

"Is there something funny?"

"Sorry, love," Sally said, wiping sleep from the corner of her eye, "How much does tha think I earn? After I've paid me mortgage, done the shoppin', then the kids have eaten all the food too quickly, once I've paid the bills, paid our Jordan's football subs, our Alice's dance classes, I ant got a penny for me sen! Never mind spending God knows how much on a return flight!"

Clarke blushed and looked down at the floor.

"No need to be embarrassed about it, love, I reckon when you've got money, it's hard to imagine life without it."

Sally unwrapped the foil of her tuna sandwich, and offered a quarter to Clarke, who declined. She took out a small flask, unscrewed the cap, and poured herself a cup of tea. The pair sat silently for the last ten minutes of her lunch break. From the edge of her vision, Sally was aware of Clarke's frequent glances towards her whilst she mused on the events of the coming evening, and whether the tuck shop she ran for her son's football team needed replenishing before the game tomorrow. Sensing that she wasn't going to get anywhere with Clarke because of their gulf of life experiences, she brushed the crumbs off her apron, and winced as her knees ached.

"If one doesn't mind me asking, how do you do it?" said Clarke suddenly.

"Do what, love?" she said, eyebrows raised.

"This!" said Clarke with a thoughtful scowl whilst pinning her hair back, "Cleaning, day in day out, in the same place for seventeen years. I suppose you get terribly bored?"

"That's what I don't get about your lot," Sally said with a snort, "You flitter between well paid jobs, tramplin' over one another to get theer. Tek most people who pass through the departures lounge, never seen such a miserable bunch, you wunt think anyone here were headin' to other worlds in an hour or two, look as if they'd bin to the supermarket and had to talk to someone! It's got nowt to do with boredom, it's part necessity."

"What do you mean, *part*?"

"Madam," said Sally, "Can I ask you summat, a personal question, seein' as you've perked up a tad?"

"I don't see why not."

"Have yer got any kids?"

Sally saw Clarke's face stiffen.

"I dint mean owt by it, love, you said it were oreyt to ask."

"Oh, no, it's fine, honestly," said Clarke, turning the red wine-stained glass through her thumb and forefinger.

"That's why I've been here so long. The hours are flexible, the pay is good, and by and large, management is fair. You need a setup like that when you've got three sparrows at home, that and our John's been in and outta' work all his life; like a lot of people I know, he works a job for a few years only to be replaced by one of them," said Sally, gesturing towards the Assistants in their charging dock.

"But didn't you ever dream of being something bigger than a cleaner? Doing something extraordinary?"

Sally laughed and picked at the sleep in her eye, flicking it onto the floor.

"Nothin' like that, love. I never really knew what I wanted to do — growin' up I guess I wanted to do somethin' with space. Growin' up seein' the Mars landings, seein' a woman, not a man, pressin' the first human footprint on to the Red Planet, well, there wasn't a girl around that dint want to do the same — but I never worked hard enough in school, and I met our John, and things just came together. That's why I've stayed here all these years I guess, cus' in some small way, I'm helpin' send humanity to the stars," she finished, staring out towards a greatship being slowly erected in the distance.

"It's quite beautiful isn't it?" said Clarke, turning to face the launch pad, "Not necessarily in the physical sense, but in its symbolism. Gosh, until you mentioned it just now, Sally, I hadn't thought about the Mars landings in such a long time. Those first images from the Red Planet: the white suits juxtaposed against the orange earth, the dark dunes and dust devils, the sweeping granules scratching the headcams, the machines that inflated into a Martian manse-"

"And the round of golf," added Sally.

"I'd forgotten all about that!" said Clarke excitedly, "Yes, yes, and how the taikonauts spent half an hour looking for the ball, all the while mission control were barking commands at them to focus."

"'Sorry, Houston, it's your fault, you should've packed a nine iron!'" they said together, snorting with laughter. Sally rubbed her callused hands and looked out on the tarmac as two shuttles with flashing, orange lights, loaded with maintenance staff, headed towards the greatship.

"I apologise if this sounds facetious," began Clarke, "but it would had never dawned on me that the pair of us would be driven by the same events — I assumed that a cleaner would be motivated, by, well, I don't know what. For some time now, when sat in spaceports, I've wondered as to why the Temex Corporation introduced maintenance jobs, when the machines were capable of cleaning and hauling baggage. But I see now why that decision was made! It's about adding-"

"So what you're sayin', madam, is that me job has no real value?"

"No, not at all!" said Clarke, her eyes widening. "That is not what I meant at all! I -"

Nodding slowly, Sally rolled her tongue over her teeth.

"Dunt matter what kind of job comes around, or why it's there, it just matters that there is a job, that there's a way to put food onto the table. Outside of this place, folks are really strugglin', and have been ever since the last colliery closed all those years ago. But what baffles me, madam, if yer don't mind me sayin', is why anyone would walk away from a well-paid job. Why did you do it? I mean, if I earnt money like that..." said Sally, puffing out her cheeks, pushing the air out slowly, thinking of the holidays she'd take, the cottage her John dreamed of buying on what was left of the Devonshire coast.

"It wasn't the money that ever bothered me, sure, I was well paid for what I did," said Clarke. "Tell me Sally, how many hours do you do a week?"

"Bang on thirty-seven, no more, no less."

"In my early years at Temex, I worked seventy, maybe eighty-hour weeks to get humanity to Ceres, and back then, the company had a vision I believed in. No one thought Ceres would be as lucrative as it was when it came to rare metal reserves. Have you heard of Promethium?"

"No."

Clarke gestured to the distant greatship on the launch pad.

"Well, without it, we wouldn't be able to make those in the quantities we do. It seemed self-perpetuating: the more greatships we made, the more people came to Ceres, and the more they realised the money to be made, legally and otherwise."

Clarke shuffled down the bench to sit closer to Sally, leaning in to whisper.

"Naturally, the stakeholders got hold of this insight, and realising the potential for

personal gain, well, plans to establish a human presence beyond the asteroid belt were soon abandoned. The types of people filtering into Temex, too, changed, from those with solar wanderlust, to the insatiably greedy, stymieing attempts to push the boundaries of civilisation."

Sally couldn't help but smile. The way Clarke spoke reminded her of John, and his great schemes that never came to fruition.

"You're like me other half, a romantic: his eyes bulge like yours when he goes off on some grand plan he's got. But I've got to ask, madam, why is thee still wearin' a Temex outfit if you hate the place so bloody much?"

"I'm just...just so lost, Sally," said Clarke with a sigh. "This is going to sound so *so* stupid, and I don't know why I'm telling a stranger this, but I've been hopping around the spaceports — my access hasn't been removed yet — watching greatship after greatship ascend to Ceres, hoping it will give me an idea of what to do, if that makes any sense?"

Sally hesitated in her reply, scanning Clarke's eyes that reminded her of someone she hadn't thought about in a long time.

"Has thee ever thought about teaching?"

"What makes you say that?" said a scowling Clarke.

"I haven't thought about this in years. My maths teacher back at school, Mrs Cook — she used to bang on to me about studyin', but I knew better at that age," said Sally.

"A wise woman by the sounds of it."

"Aye, well, I asked her once why she taught us lot, a bunch of rowdy kids, instead of doin' summat else. She said 'because I worked for so long somewhere earning good money, but absolutely hating every minute of it, I were miserable, and forgot why I studied maths in the first place.' It's funny how some words stay with yer."

Sally exhaled as her watch beeped, marking the end of her break. Below, passengers began to flood into the departures lounge for the three o'clock flight. As she stood up, placing her palms on her aching knees, she sensed a loneliness in Clarke: a person whose life had pivoted around a company, where pushing others away in pursuit of high achievement was to be admired — it wouldn't surprise Sally if during her working life no one had asked Clarke if she was alright, if she had any plans for the weekend. This shouldn't have saddened Sally as much as it did. She stared at this strong and intelligent woman, who had sat silent for most of Sally's lunch break, shifting from being almost offended, to utterly disarmed.

"I'm sorry love, really, I've gorra' get back to work, I've got the third-tier toilets to do."

"Wait," said Clarke, grabbing her wrist. "Wait, Sally, what time do you finish?"

"Five o'clock, why?"

"Just meet me by the spaceport entrance, promise me."

Naturally suspicious, Sally pulled her wrist away, and tucked it into her apron. She'd only just met this woman, and in almost two decades toiling away in Barnsley One, nothing like this had ever happened. She held Clarke's gaze, searching for the kind of misdirection she'd seen so many times in the eyes of her children.

"Oreyt then, love," said Sally. "I guess I'll see you then."

Whilst typing in the code to her locker, Sally felt an earthquake. Knocked to the floor, she pulled her legs into a foetal position, protecting her head as the pre-fabricated walls of the staff room bent inwards, letting loose picture frames and graphene screens. The room swayed, as did time, reminding Sally of the times she'd failed to properly synchronise the gyroscopes in her son's virtual reality headset. When all was still, she stood up, brushed fragments of safety glass from her apron, and headed to the departures lounge.

A sprawling crack had weaved itself across the dome. Hundreds of onlookers gawped at the felled giant with its sparking veins, as it disappeared behind a descending shield protecting the glass dome from debris. Over the sound of her thrumming eardrums, it took her a minute to realise the evacuation alarms were waning. High visibility jackets burst into the departure lounge accompanied by Assistants, their porcelain white shells replaced by a throbbing amber. With the spaceport in lockdown, dazed passengers were ushered away with little resistance into the foyer.

"You bastards!" spat a man in his mid-forties, pointing his index finger at Sally. "My colleague was on that shuttle — why won't you confirm what's happening? Have you no soul?"

"We're mekin' sense of the situation, we ask yer to be patient. The Temex Corporation will keep yer up to date with the developments," said Sally for the tenth time in as many minutes. Everyone knew the outcome regardless of Temex's hesitance. Although safety standards were constantly improving, the odds of walking away from a ten-megaton explosion, regardless of all the safety features, were zero. Two more hours passed by, and as per lockdown procedures, Sally stood there with her hands clasped against the small of her back against the giant pneumatic doors that led to the departures lounge.

"Excuse me, I'm going to need to come past."

Looking up from her feet, Sally was surprised to see Clarke. She smiled faintly, but there seemed to be no recognition. Huffing in frustration, the First Officer moved past Sally, aligned her face with a scanner, and squeezed through the emerging gap in the hissing doors. Clarke's colleagues snaked around Sally like ducklings behind their matriarch, uninterested in the obstruction. Given the situation, it shouldn't have surprised Sally that Clarke had forgotten all about her, though that didn't stop her feeling that she'd been misled; if anything, it confirmed her suspicions that Clarke had never intended to meet with her after work. In the thick humidity of Barnsley One's foyer,

the air conditioning having been knocked out due to a power surge, Sally rolled up her heavy sleeve, pretended to check her watch, glanced at a security detail arguing with a swelling group of furious detainees, and made her escape to the water cooler. Her head swaying with dehydration, she hobbled through the sombre crowd; many people slumped around piles of crumpled jackets and discarded ties as they watched the Prime Minister's press conference on the disaster.

"It's disgusting that we have to hear the Prime Minister tell us that there have been no survivors rather than the Temex executive — it's an absolute shambles," muttered a passenger as Sally headed back to her post, a plastic cup of water in hand.

"And their staff are just lazing around, what are they even paying them for?" said another, making eye contact with Sally. To prevent a flippant remark, she had to bite the corner of her mouth so hard that her incisor pierced the skin. A moment of bitterness overcame Sally. Unlike Clarke, she couldn't just fly off the hook, couldn't just walk away and resign, or fly around the world's spaceports aimlessly waiting for something interesting to happen; for all the woman's impressive academic and professional achievements, her roots were shallow, neglected in the summer sun, whilst Sally's were tendered well by her neighbours and family, stretching far below the South Yorkshire soil, their tendrils rooted deep below in the mantle.

"Where have you been e00837?" said Malcolm, or a proper jobsworth as Sally liked to think of him, with his clipboard and combover.

"Don't start with me love, I just went to get some bloody water, does tha' want me to collapse?" she said flicking her hand in the air. "It's criminal to mek staff stand here when tha's got all those bloody Assistant's doin' nowt!"

Sally liked to rile Malcom, and as his face reddened, a Temex official entered the room, and called for the attention of passengers.

"About bloody time," murmured Sally to herself, as Malcolm backed away, gesturing that he was watching her. Apologising for the delay, the official outlined the reasons for the shutdown protocol, provided an estimated time of escape, and re-iterated the words of the Prime Minister.

"Yes, sir, I appreciate your frustration, but we've had to re-route the power supply away from non-essential units, which, sadly, does include the air conditioning."

"Of course you'll be refunded, madam."

"With regards to 'psychological damages' I couldn't possibly comment as I'm not a qualified clinician."

The loaded questions carried on for fifteen minutes, until the official was ushered away by security to a chorus of booing. The air muggy and solid, many passengers deflated back into the metal folds of chairs, chatting quietly and consoling the few that had lost close friends and relatives.

On the back of eight o'clock came the announcement that the lockdown was over. A plastic tunnel had been erected over the entrance to Barnsley One's foyer that was soon flooded with two lanes of traffic and a weary-looking contingent of Temex professionals arriving, jostling.

Soon relieved from her role, and unexpectedly praised by her manager for her diligence, Sally hurried back to the locker in the departures lounge and retrieved her belongings, quickly called her husband John, attending to his twelve missed calls, and crossed the foyer to leave for the night. As she turned into the tunnel, she noticed a single woman sat there, her mauve jacket folded over her lap, thin red marks stretched down her face. Turning on her heels, she headed towards her.

"Are you oreyt there love?" said Sally to the lone woman on the bench, "Do yer want me to come and set with yer?"

The woman extended a hand, lined with liver spots and

wrinkles that reminded Sally of her grandfather.

"Ruth. You're a good 'un love, but are you sure? Ever so kind of you to offer. You must be knackered."

"Don't worry about me."

In her early sixties, with blonde hair tied up in a bun, Ruth smiled weakly and looked at the floor whilst brushing a tear away with a fist. Sally took out her flask from her apron, tapping the bottom of it to push out the last dregs of tea.

"Sorry love, it's a bit cold, haven't had chance to top it up."

"Ta."

Sally pressed the cup into Ruth's shaking palms, and gently squeezed her forearm, soon slowing the tremor.

"I can't believe it...I can't believe our Steven has..."

Ruth's shoulders shook; she let go of Sally's palm, firmly brushing her tears away, as if trying to buff the red streaks from her cheekbones.

"I'm sorry for your loss, love, I mean it, I can't imagine what yer goin' through — and when I say this, I'm not tryna' get rid of yer, but is anyone comin' to pick yer up? This int a place to be sat alone."

"My other half is on his way," she said with a sniffle, "Shouldn't be more than twenty minutes — he's insisted on coming in his gasoline, the man's more stubborn than seagull, he's never trusted those flying transits that drive themselves — I'm not in the mood for arguing."

"Aye, don't get me started on men."

It turned half nine when Sally left. She made her way to the rapid transit shuttle, covering her nose and mouth to try and block the pungent smell of fuel. Emotionally and physically exhausted, she slumped into the single seated drone, inhaled its dry, odourless air, punched in her postcode, and let the tears fall.

Two months had passed by since her chance encounter with Clarke, and Sally, apart from the rest over the Easter bank holiday, grafted as tirelessly as ever. One winter evening, taking the rapid transit home, which weaved through rows of red brick 1960s council houses, she finally arrived, threw her sodden rain mac over the banister rail, and shuffled her feet on the welcome mat, closing the door behind her.

"Hello, love," shouted John from the kitchen, "Fancy a brew?"

"Aye, that'd be nice."

"Oh, and Sal," he said, emerging with a tea towel cast over his shoulder, "I had to sign for your delivery this afternoon after I got back from the job centre, it's on the table in the lounge. What is it, love?"

"Funny that, 'cos I haven't ordered owt. Is our Jordan in?"

"Aye, but he says it's nowt to do with him."

Frowning, she sifted through the wicker drawers, turning over odd gloves and bare rolls of sellotape, before taking out a pair of scissors.

"Ta, love," said Sally, kissing her husband on the cheek. John placed the steaming mug of tea next to the box, and with a deft flick, she struck open the package, peered inside, and began to laugh.

"What's got you?"

From the box, Sally pulled out a heavy woven rainbow-coloured poncho, and a silver-plated box bearing the emblem of the Temex Corporation. The magnolia walls recoiled as she swung the poncho over her head. A letter fell to the carpet. *For Sally*.

"And thee keeps goin' on about how I've got a bad taste in fashion!"

Sally punched John playfully as he knelt down with his hand on his back and passed her the envelope. Perching on the edge of the settee, she slurped at her tea, dug her fingernail under the seal, took another gulp, and slid out a handwritten letter.

"Bit weak this, love," she said, cocking her head towards her tea.

"Never mind that, what I want to know is whys thee's gone so quiet — if there's a secret to it, I want to know."

"Is thee after a divorce?" said Sally, as she began to read:

Sally,

I hope this letter finds you in good health. You might not remember me, I expect, working in such a transient setting — when we met I was most unkind in the face of your concern, acting a little like a spoilt teenager, though I hope you'll forgive me.

The children helped to not only knit the poncho, but clearly, were involved in the design process, and I for one rather like it. Until we'd met, I'm ashamed to say, I cannot say I'd ever interacted with anyone from a background so different from my own; your words have stuck with me: 'it doesn't matter what kind of job comes around, or why it's there, it just matters that there is a job, that there's a way to put food onto the table'. It made me think about how privileged I've been, and that perhaps my sudden change in circumstance could be a chance to give something back. I'd never considered teaching before our exchange — coincidently, an old college friend of mine, Lu, got in touch that evening after our encounter, enquiring about my health, after seeing me on a broadcast about the disaster.

I write this letter to you from a school in Mumbai, where I've been working for two months now, and teaching, alongside Lu, all kinds of inspiring young people that have suffered great hardships, though maintain a most wonderful resilience, and an insatiable love of learning...and creativity.

I'm sorry that we weren't able to meet that afternoon, and that I didn't write this letter sooner. I was concerned that after the tragedy that unfolded that day, you may not have appreciated my gift in the silver box. At the very moment of teetering over an insurmountable void, you came along and asked me if I was alright, if I wanted to talk, if I wanted a piece of your sandwich, you eased me with your contentedness; you have no idea what those moments did for me. As I sat there in silence watching you sip your flask of tea, I was struck by an overwhelming desire to be the person to give you the childlike eyes of those first civilians that boarded a greatship to Ceres....

"Bloody 'ell," said John, opening the silver box. "Bloody 'ell."

Shaken and distant, he fell back into the armchair. In his quivering hands he clutched two wafer thin screens: a pair of return tickets to Ceres.

"You've got some reyt explain' to do, Sal."

THE END

SUGAR GLASS

Elaine Roberts

Hello boys and girls. My name is Jeff. And to make sugar glass, you first dissolve sugar in a vat of water. Then you heat it to at least the *hard crack* stage. That's 150°C. After it cools you form it into a sheet that resembles a window pane, you swaddle your giant, translucent newborn in bubble wrap, you drive it to the studios, and voila. Bond escapes his nemesis via closed window once again. A hurried reaction shot, a scream from a supporting actor — sometimes that makes the cut, sometimes it's replaced with a Wilhelm. That's all done after I've gone home anyway. Then it's a new day, a new set, more sugar glass, lather, rinse, repeat.

Until today. My last day. Forty years, and my final job is for the band Disciples of Hades. They call themselves "musicians" and were one of my son's favourites. I insisted that the retirement kerfuffle happen ahead of the shoot rather than some inappropriately raucous affair afterwards. *No fuss, no fuss please* I begged, so the director just gave a short speech and we promptly started work on building the set, which is school-corridor-meets-Victorian-funeral. I caught the rueful smiles and sympathetic head tilts from the rest of the crew. It's only been five months since I lost my son, and I'm at the tail

end of that special treatment one receives after a bereavement. He would have been seventeen this week.

"Jeff! Nearly ready?" The director's face hovers above mine.

"Almost done, mate. This one's fiddly."

"Don't mess up your final job, will you? Ha!"

Forty years of moulding the putty in my hands first — that makes it soft — then running it around the frame, and finally — carefully — wiggling the stunt glass into place. Countless film sets, theatre sets, music videos like today. A high-speed chase, or a fight in a high-rise, then *pow* — our villain or hero sinks through the sugar glass and plunges all the way down to a mattress — three feet below.

What a shame I forgot the sugar glass today.

I panicked at first, when I remembered I had to get my real pane past the band's security — *ay, there's the rub* — but those Neanderthal fools ushered through the forty-years-in-the job old boy with some shitty joke about feeling *shattered*.

While the crew dance around, tweaking the lighting and polishing props, I slowly get to my feet (my knees crack) to admire my final piece of handiwork. The pane shines above me, flawless, magnificent, the foil on a coffee jar waiting to be broken.

"All in place now, chief."

"Excellent! Come on Jeff, stay for one beer afterwards?"

Dangerous, the whole damn band. Using their fame and so-called talent to push their romanticised ideas about death onto young minds. That screaming excuse for music, those infernal tattoos and piercings, their lyrics about *cutting* and *choking* and *slitting*. Now they'll have to cope with real blood, real pain, like I had to — thanks to them. I wonder what they'll do when their lead yowler is haemorrhaging down the corridor?

"No, chief. Sorry. Thanks for everything."

"But—"

It's too late. By the time the stars of the show are ushered onto set, I'm already driving, aching for justice, and hurtling towards infamy and oblivion.

THE END

THE UNDATED LAMINGTON LETTERS

Aizuddin H. Anuar

Dear Kay,

You were always the most responsible among us. I knew I could always trust you to do the right thing. Whenever we became quiet, buried beneath the weight of schoolwork or distracted by newly-formed friendships in different circles, you could always be counted on to pull us back together.

I remember once you planned a barbeque catch up at the park on Maroubra Beach, meticulously emailing everyone his or her roles, the date and time, the weather forecast. You brought chicken wings and sausages from that halal butcher in Kensington where you worked part-time to support your family back home. V and I prepared egg salad and cut-up fruits that we kept in the fridge the night before. I remember the cold wind that threw our plates in the air like whirring Frisbees, and the stray dogs that lingered for the smell of sizzling sausages. But it was a fun day out. We all made an effort. It made me think of us as those innocent kids, just arriving from a faraway land, filled with innocence and careless laughter, drawn to each other if only for the familiar language that we spoke.

This was before the realities of being international students hardened us, moulding us into different people in the process.

It pains me to recall that time on the bus when you told me that lamingtons were not halal. We never really had much common ground; there was a respectful stiffness that propped up our friendship. So, in my attempt at small talk, I shared, quite randomly, that I had bought a few boxes of this chocolate and coconut indulgence on sale at the local store. The eating of lamingtons was one of the few Australian activities that I was a party to, and your statement felt like an attack on my nascent sense of identity (you said they contain marshmallow, but I eventually realised not all of them do!). I responded weakly with a hollow gasp, and that was that. We did not speak of the matter again.

The truth is that later than night, in the darkness of my studio apartment, I finished all the lamington fingers in one sitting. I thought I would feel comforted by this act of destruction, the devouring of the edible evidence, the discreet disposal of the empty boxes in the garbage chute afterwards. Instead, I felt sick, and in the middle of the night I sat by the toilet bowl, purging myself of the sacrilege. I stayed in bed the next day and didn't turn up for classes. It was more dramatic than it needed to be now that I think of it, and it makes me smile.

What I didn't tell you is that in the many years that followed our first year here, I kept on buying lamingtons, all the while praying to God that I wouldn't bump into you in the act. I went through great lengths to avoid you, and only you, whenever I was out on a lamington run.

I don't know why I felt compelled to confess this matter to you, and I hope you don't think less of me beyond this revelation. I have always admired your uncomplicated sense of integrity, and looking at where you are now, it seems to have served you well. You know — though you pretend otherwise — that I hold your opinion of me in the highest esteem. How does that song go? *When I'm gone, please speak well of me.*

Your friend,
Adam

Dear Nishi,

What I remember most about you is your clueless sense of time. It was as if yours operated on an entirely different scale. The first few times, it had been charming: you would apologise profusely with amusing tales in tow. I decided to overlook this flaw because I had just arrived and was in dire need of a friend. I was surprised that you, of all people, had obliged. When I first met you I thought of you as somehow set apart from the rest of us. You often floated around in our classes before the professors arrived, laughing, pulling your hair away from your delicate face as you nodded, as if paying close attention to what was said. You were generous with hugs. I recall your habit of accosting random strangers in the elevator of the library or on the busy university mall just to ask them where they got their gladiator sandals, or how they did their hair in a certain way. I'm not sure why, but I always felt second-hand embarrassment every time this happened. Also, you might not know that I know this, or even remember, but once I caught you photocopying the notes I had painstakingly prepared for our open book exam, and I pretended like it didn't bother me. I conjured excuses on your behalf. Maybe you were overwhelmed by personal issues, maybe you were having trouble with multivariable calculus, maybe your lecture notes had in fact been eaten by your dog.

In my second year, I remember that we made plans to have chaat and rasmalai at that little place in Surry Hills (Maya?). We agreed to meet at the bus stop on Anzac Parade. I waited for about an hour, and in the meantime I managed to wolf down the bag of lamingtons I bought at Coles earlier. I eventually gave up when you were a no-show, after my persistent calls to your mobile went unanswered. I returned home, bloated from an improper dinner (of lamingtons!) and frustrated by your unreliable timing. I gave up. I told myself I would never tolerate your bullshit again.

A few hours later, you returned my call. When I ignored your calls, you left a long, scathing message. It was unkind of me I know, exacting revenge in that way. If my memory serves me right, you referred to me then as selfish, weird and overly emotional for a guy. The next time we met in class, we pretended our little tiff had never happened, and we skipped the three-hour practical afterwards in favour of Maya. That escapade was my initiation into the exotic world of Indian delicacies, and a few years later, when I finally visited Delhi, and I found myself incredibly overwhelmed by the wall of people and the panoply of smells and sounds, I went looking for samosa chaat, rasmalai and gulab jamun in honour of our complicated friendship.

I just wanted to thank you for being my friend at a strange time in my life. I know we eventually lost touch once we both made our way out into the world. But I have to tell you that I still think fondly of you, especially when I'm in the mood for Indian food on long, lonely nights. I hope you are on your way to somewhere great, and I hope you arrive on time, because chances in life don't often have much patience for those who are late!

Yours,
Adam

Dear Prof. Buckings,

It is my utmost hope that this letter finds you well, so I find peace in the knowledge that at least one of us is.

I don't know if it was apparent to you then, but I'm grateful that you decided to take a chance on me as I approached the end of my undergraduate studies. I don't recall much about our supervisions. A classmate told me that you spoke of me in glowing terms to other students under your care. It's funny because in my presence you always seemed so cold; I could never tell if I was making any sense to you. But like I said, I'm grateful.

What I do remember vividly is your son. Once, when I was late for our appointment, emerging with my hair still wet from the last-minute shower, dog-eared psychology journals sticking to my sweaty palms, Tom was the first to make eye contact. He was sitting in your usual spot behind the desk. I thought I had the wrong room and almost backed out. He stared at me intensely. Those eyes were full of wonder. It is a kind of veneer that ebbs with age. He offered me a half-eaten lamington finger, and you seemed surprised by this friendly gesture. I politely refused. Tom shrugged, unperturbed by the rejection, and continued with his homework. I felt my stomach twist as I took my seat opposite him, turning slightly to the side to face you. I immediately regretted not taking your son up on the offer. The hot morning sun brought in long shadows from the eucalyptus trees outside; they danced hypnotically on the mottled pages of the journals I placed between us. I felt my head spinning.

Tom commanded the desk before him, enjoying the high-backed swivel chair and the academic air. You, on the other hand, seemed dwarfed and slightly comical on the steel fold-up chair, your long legs crossing awkwardly, short of touching

mine. We continued our session like any other, as if both of us had not been disoriented even in the slightest. You probed with more questions instead of giving any straightforward guidance for my research project, and that annoyed me. From the corner of my eye, I caught Tom peeking into our conversation, returning abruptly to his maths homework whenever I stole a glance at him, smiling conspiratorially at our little game. Before I left your office, I relented when Tom once again offered me the Lamington finger. You insisted on it. You must have heard the grumbling of my stomach earlier, which I thought I had only imagined in my mind.

That was the only time I ever saw Tom in person. Years later, after I had left Australia, I once again caught sight of that pair of eyes as I scrolled through your Facebook page, immediately after you had approved my friend request. There are many pictures of him uploaded by your wife, tagging you and her other relatives on photo albums of trips to Coogee Beach, junior cricket games on the university green and outdoor art festivals at Darling Harbour. He was of course older, but those eyes, looking into the camera, sometimes distractedly, sometimes intensely, transported me to the first time I saw him in your office many years before.

I hope he grows up to be someone you are proud of. I think that's all that parents want in the end, much like mine, though I cannot say with a clear conscience that their wish was fulfilled.

My very best wishes,
Adam Abdul Majid

Dear V,

My Australian adventure was characterized chiefly by your ubiquitous presence throughout. Even now, when my memory is becoming fuzzy, blurred by all the medicine and tinged with uncontrollable nostalgia, you are a constant figure in every frame. I don't see much point in writing to you; what I have to say has already been said. We arrived together, we departed together, though in the truest sense, we departed from each other.

But do you remember how we lived in the library, every single year around study breaks before mid-term exams? I recall this so vividly. We trudged up there together, braving the howling winds that coursed through the vacant buildings, our scarves tucked into the front of our flapping coats, chatting all the way, shivering to our bones. Despite warnings, we smuggled in our flasks of mushroom soup (from the can), Starburst jelly beans that stained our tongues, home-made fried rice with cut-up sausages. The alien smells wafted about, punctuating the studious air. We stayed on long after others had retired home, when the stacks and aisles stood glumly and lonely. The tall, imposing library building — visible on clear days from some parts of the Centennial Park — sighed contentedly in the pitch dark. We never got much studying done. We loved watching communitychannel on YouTube, sharing a pair of earphones, stifling laughter until our stomachs hurt. In quieter moments, we recollected our shared past and speculated about the great future, its shape at that time unknown to the both of us.

After you broke up with David, you went on a crying spell. Have I ever told you it was so intense that it frightened me? It washed over me as an intimacy I was honestly not prepared for. I could tell at first you pretended you were strong enough to face the dissolution of young love. We still went out for our Sunday morning brunches at Coogee Beach, though my salmon eggs Benedict seemed out of place without your usual buttermilk pancakes. You sat there vacantly, your eyes puffy from tears, staring out into the ocean, smiling slightly at my lame jokes. Our protracted silence was broken rhythmically by the crashing waves before us, and that gave me some relief. Then there were the aimless walks through Centennial Park. One time we wandered through the lush greenery all the way to Oxford St and into Paddington, mostly silent all the way; hushed tears were shed on your part. I learned then the fundamental value of abiding, of standing inaudibly with you, of being by and on your side, jointly enduring this shapeless pain without offering any solution. You had not expected me to.

I was not surprised when you were quick to reciprocate this gesture while we were in the thick of that great future, years later, at a time that I needed you most. When whatever future I had planned for was cut short, when promises buoyed by all this potential were broken unannounced. When my life spiralled out of my power, eclipsed by His Grand Design.

When the tiny particulates of sand that made evident my bodily existence—from Bondi to Coogee to Maroubra to Manly to Clovelly to all the other great beaches of my life—were all slipping through my fingers, leaving me little by little.

Now, V, with time running out, I have to ask one last favour of you. On the one-year anniversary of my departure, once "too soon" is no more, bring these letters, and read them in this order, out loud, to my mother. Recently, in passing, she told me — in a wistful tone that was not lost on me — how hollow she had felt when I fled to Australia. Always wondering what I was up to, hungry for any semblance of connection across the big, tumultuous sea.

I hope this peek into what was once my life will bring her some catharsis. And though it is such a difficult task to ask of you, V, I pray it will bring you some relief, too. I've been told that *with every difficulty there is relief, with every difficulty there is relief.* I have to believe this to be true.

Forever yours,

A

P/S: Are you still watching communitychannel on YouTube? I think I will literally die before she ever makes that lamingtons recipe video!

THE END

THIS SONG IS ALL ABOUT WAR

'Doc' David

"This song is all about war," said the very skinny Vivien to the very drunk Fisher at the table next to the jukebox. The song about war is Born In The USA. The song excites Fisher, and he bounces his feet in his chair and makes noises that approximate the sounds of the song. "*Bruce Springsteen is The Boss!*" he simpers. Vivien stops feeding coins into the jukebox and sits down on a chair close to Fisher, letting him stroke her short hair and say things like Bruce Springsteen is The Boss. Then, when the song is finished, it starts again, and so does Fisher. Born In The USA. A song about war.

The Anchor Inn is situated at the end of Anchor Lane, off the High Street. The snow is falling, sluicing the sky like soft wet shoes. The evening draws to a premature close, but Mitchell doesn't seem to notice. He is understated and underdressed in his blue jeans and just a t-shirt, a picture of Status Quo on the front of the shirt, a cracking gig souvenir from two years back.

He's on his way over to the Anchor from the Oranges

and Lemons, via the Gloucester Arms, whose jukeboxes are conducive to the quaffing of ale. As is the Anchor's. He pauses beneath the centuries old Carfax Tower, looking up to check the time on the big clock. All around is the buzz of the weekend, the trail of car headlights through the snow and the students waving bottles of plonk as they pass him by, one ubiquitous landmark to another. "I am very pleased," says Mitchell, doffing a pretend hat to the lovely ladies.

Mitchell never went to university. He sometimes wonders what it would have been like if he had, and drives miles out of his way on errands, taking the work's pickup and making a circuit of the University of Oxford to see what he is missing. To rub his own nose in it. *That's not easy*, he thinks to himself, placing the pretend hat back on his head. But he rolls with the punches, like Marc Bolan and T.Rex. Get it on, bang a gong.

He is snapped from his reverie by a small group of women wanting directions to a decent pub. They are bubbly and from out of town, sheepskin coats and handbags against the snow. Mitchell looks at them, up and down. "Love the accent," he says. "That will do 100 percent. Shake your hand," and he gives the girl asking the questions his hand. She's got a lovely hand. He asks what they do and where they are from and they say what sounds like Gal, which is in Wales.

"Gal like girl," sniffs Mitchell. He tells them about the Anchor, which is where he is headed. They walk with him as he points out the sights of Oxford. The Town Hall is on the right, and that place next to it is a university. They walk daintily, touching a wall for steady progress.

He tells them about the good jukebox in the Anchor, about Jethro Tull and Living In The Past, and the Quo's Sweet Caroline. They like a good jukebox, the girls agree.

"Gal," Mitchell reminds them. He's never been there. He doesn't know Wales too well and tells the girls from Gal all about it. "I got no problem with the Welsh," he decides and wonders what good bands are from Wales. Then he remembers that he's got no problems with the Welsh, although some of his friends have got *major* problems with the Welsh. He begins to list those problems and those of the people who live on the Isle of Man.

"Manx," says the girl with the lovely hand.

"Manx," repeats Mitchell. "Thank you. Well done. Well done."

The girls don't go to the Anchor after that, leaving Mitchell to make his own way down Anchor Lane, off the High Street. He shrugs. Come the morning he may not remember any of this, so no point in fretting about it.

The thumping bass line of Born In The USA filters through the alleyway. *This is what matters*, thinks Mitchell, spreading his arms and placing a hand on either side of the alley walls. As was the case with Carfax Tower, he lets the moment come to him, to be one with it.

Fisher is at a loss as to what comes next, so Vivien attracts the attention of another man, who looks up from the book he is reading. She waves her hand. *Yes, I can see you*, thinks the man, *you are all of five feet away. Can you see me?* She heads toward him, navigating a table and chairs with her twisting hips.

"What are you reading?" she asks. The man flips the book over to its cover and shows it to Vivien. It is a primer for teaching the alphabet to young children.

"Ah, good book!" Vivien declares. "Great book. I've read that!"

The man thinks it unlikely.

She is still looking at the cover of the book when she says that she and Fisher are having a "set-to", tipping her head in the direction of the man who likes the Boss, now smoking a roll up. Vivien smiles and suddenly pulls herself erect.

"My name is Lt Vivien Daily," she declares, and offers a hand to the stranger that is small and cramped with booze. He wonders whether to take the hand and shake it or to salute her. There isn't much else after that, and Vivien cheerily heads back the way she had come through the bar room.

"Good book, I've read it," she says again.

Fisher is now involved with an empty bottle of Newcastle Brown Ale, which he places on the table, adding it to other bottles of Newcastle Brown Ale, all empty. The dancing moves have left him and he is thirsty again. He calls over to the old woman at a far table, another regular. Old Mother, he calls her. The reason everyone is in the pub is because it is Old Mother's birthday. But everyone is always in the pub. Old Mother is pulling a purse from her handbag, like the purse of a doll. She takes pennies from it and places them carefully on the table. It is her birthday, she says, and she insists on buying everyone a drink. She has not enough money to buy everyone a drink and so she counts out the money again. Vivien heads over, rubbing her hands together and taking her time.

"Mother," says Vivien. "Put your money away."

Old Mother is too busy to notice and makes a face to suggest she is too busy to notice and another face that cannot be distracted. Vivien sits at the table and watches Old Mother displacing the coins, and commences to tell her a story about a landlord of a pub not a million miles away who fancies the boys. The landlord who fancies the boys carries a packet of jam tarts for emergencies.

"Where'd he get the jam tarts?" Old Mother asks, pushing coins around the table.

Vivien contemplates the question because it is probably significant. "Sainbury's," she says at last.

"The landlord had jam tarts," Vivien continues the story. "He kept a packet of them behind the bar. Then he snapped open the packet, saying he deserved them with the day he's had." Vivien leans closer with the secrets. "When the boys come in, he offers them one. A jam tart. And when they leave, he says don't do anything I wouldn't do. *Don't do anything I wouldn't do!*"

Old Mother stops counting and looks at Vivien closely.

"Fisher told me," Vivien says by way of an explanation. "His eyes were red and searching their trousers."

"Fisher's eyes are always red," Old Mother snorts, looking across at the figure slumped by the jukebox, surrounded by empty bottles of Newcastle Brown Ale.

"Not Fisher's eyes!" That is the damnedest thing Vivien has ever heard. "The landlord's eyes! The landlord's eyes were red! I just told you! And then he says 'would you like a jam tart.'"

The man with the book has closed his book and is leaving. "Goodbye Lt Vivien Daily," he calls from the door. Vivien waves absently to him and goes back over to Fisher, who is unhappy about the jukebox because the Boss is gone, replaced by music he does not like. She attempts to console him but his mincing attitude bothers her terribly.

"Listen," snaps Vivien. "I'm not a fan of New Order, you know what I'm talking about."

Fisher nods, making sense of it.

"I'm not a fan of New Order." She gets back up and waves a finger at Fisher from across the table. "I don't care for New Order."

Fisher concedes defeat, raising his hands heavily. Vivien might die if she fails to deliver a manifesto before nightfall, such is her manner. But he still prefers the Boss and songs about war.

A man enters the pub at that moment with a pint of milk

in one hand and a cane in the other. He has a funny hat on his head and he walks neatly to the bar. A girl follows him soon afterwards. She looks less than half his age, yet their body language is intimate.

"Where you going with that?" Vivien asks about the milk.

"This here is my friend Sandra Setters," responds the man with the milk. "All the S's. We are headed off in a minute. We're having a pint and we're off."

The man places the milk on the bar. "This is milk," he says, and Sandra giggles. He orders a pint of mild for himself and something for the lady. Another pint of mild. Then he looks over at Vivien and Fisher and over at the old woman still counting coins. "First we are going to the Uffington White Horse and when we return, a bottle of wine with the missus," Sandra pushes his arm fiercely. Somebody claps. "We've got salad and we'll see what happens."

Sandra says, "What are you like?"

But Vivien and Fisher are off the reservation by this point. She asks him one difficult question too many, and then wonders aloud whether they are having a good time.

"We are having a good time," responds Fisher, his words a hurried mess.

Over the Falls, off the reservation.

Vivien gets up for the bar but returns soon after empty-handed.

"They are not serving us," she says plaintively. "We are too drunk."

Too drunk? Fisher looks at Vivien for a long time after that, unable to fathom the emotion required of him. He looks at the cropped hair and curves grown old and he looks over at Old Mother and the man with milk at the bar. He doesn't look at the landlord.

Vivien gets up to feed the jukebox, choosing more songs

by the Boss and some by Little Stevie Wonder. Sandra Setters starts to dance with the music, and Mitchell, arriving at the pub, pushing open the door and calling out for a bit of Quo, watches the girl dance like he's watching the Northern Lights.

He's forgotten about it now, the memory swallowed by the many facets of pub and booze, but he met them all on that nocturnal walkabout.

Mitchell is talking to Sandra and he's talking to the old man, whose name is Baker, and he's talking to Vivien and she to Fisher — as much as anyone can talk to Fisher the state he's in. He's had a skinful. He's twatted. It fucking is. It's fucking awkward. Mitchell keeps saying Quo and Fisher keeps singing a song about war. Awkward Fisher, Mitchell talking. He pushes Fisher and Fisher pushes back. *Why are we fucking talking like this?* debates Mitchell. Vivien interjects: I know you smoke a bit of weed, she says to Fisher, shaking Fisher by the shoulders to get him to his toes. But it doesn't happen in the house — *end of*, she says. The weed. Lay down the basics, Sandra tells Vivien. The ground rules. Not in the house. Washing work clothes separately still full of fucking wet clothes. Fucking seriously! Wash them again, freshen them up for your own good.

Vivien looks to the pub for an opinion. Mr Baker knows about washing. He says that Fisher looks like he's using a lot of fabric conditioner.

The piano solo at the end of Layla is playing on the jukebox.

These are the best days of our lives, volunteers Vivien, who then starts to cry.

Don't worry about it, Fisher consoles her in a moment of alacrity. It's the piano solo at the end of Layla that divides opinion. He likes The Boss. The end bit in Layla on the other hand, the boring bit, his new friend Mitchell likes, like it's familiar for him to like it, clever or sentimental. He on the other hand does not like it. Piano keys. Fisher moves his fingers as if summertime has arrived at the invisible keyboard.

Sandra says she's going to a seminar at uni tomorrow as Mr Baker returns to the bar for more drinks. He doesn't think another drink will hurt. The barrel's being changed, he's informed by a barman who checks the £5 note handed to him. He and the barman wait for the barrel to be changed, during which time Mr Baker tells everyone about the Uffington White Horse, where he and Sandra are going imminently. He has nothing good to say about having to wait at the bar for the barrel to be changed.

It could be worse, says Mitchell.

Aye. Touch wood, I'm still alive, says Mr Baker, tapping the bar with the top of his cane. He explains to all the burial mound that is ancient, near to the Uffington White Horse. Mitchell knows it for sure.

THE END

WAVE SONG

C. B. Blakey

To another person, the sound in the earphones might have just been static, but Maris knew it was different. The roar and hiss brought a sense of belonging, a path to a place where the wind tugged at her clothes and she could taste salt on the air. As she listened, the keyboard seemed to distort beneath her fingers, the edges becoming rounded and irregular, the surfaces gritty with sand.

Someone was speaking, the words stretched and blurred by distance — then a hand touched her shoulder and jolted her from her reverie. Maris tugged out an earphone and stared up into the face of her manager.

"You ok, Maris?" Jane's voice was laced with concern, but a small frown had twitched into place over her glasses, a sure sign she was irritated.

Maris nodded. Her fingers were fidgeting with the edge of her keyboard and she balled her hands into fists to still them.

Jane stared down at her for a moment, the slim jaw tightening. Then she gave a little shrug and stepped back to where she must have standing when she first spoke. "Have you finished the minutes? From this morning?"

Maris blinked and glanced at the clock, her stomach

sinking as she registered the time. She hesitated, then raised her hands and signed her response. *Sorry. Tomorrow?* Maris kept the movements slow, fighting to keep her fingers from twitching anxiously. Jane shook her head.

"That won't do Maris, you said I'd have them this afternoon."

Sorry. Maris's fingers fluttered swiftly. She paused, then tried again. *Sorry. Tomorrow morning. I'll stay late.*

Jane let out a slow breath. "Fine, send them over before you head home." Jane turned to head back to her office, then paused. "You should turn the music down. If you can't hear when people are speaking to you it's probably bad for your ears."

Maris watched as Jane stalked away, then turned back to stare blankly at the screen. She supposed Jane meant well. In truth she was a good manager; there weren't many who'd learn basic sign language for the sake of one employee.

Jane couldn't be expected to understand this, though. The music wasn't too loud, it wasn't playing at all. Maris was listening to the silence, to the space below the silence where the sounds rose just at the edge of hearing. Maris was listening to the waves.

She had first heard it a month ago, the faintest hiss of surf lingering after her playlist ended. It would have been easy to dismiss it as static, but something made her increase the volume, her excitement building as the sounds came into focus. She did not realise then how the waves would come to dominate her thoughts, but as the days went by her carefully crafted playlists became increasingly redundant and her motivation faded with them. Now, four weeks later, she sat motionless before her keyboard as the office emptied around her.

No-one paid any mind to the silent girl. That was fine, she had always preferred her own company. Once all of her co-workers had departed she cleared her desk and drawers, the rustle and scratch of paper oddly magnified in the silence.

Maris knew Jane would be angry tomorrow, but that was unavoidable. There were some things that you just had to do.

After gathering her belongings, she left the office without a backwards glance.

At the pool, Maris changed slowly, enjoying the privacy of the cubicle. She twisted her waist-length black hair into a thick cord before tying it into a tight bun and donning the swimming costume. It was her most prized possession; a sleek one-piece, tight as a second skin, that shone like quicksilver in the artificial light of the pool. She ran her fingers over the shoulder straps, settling into it, admiring the way it felt. It might show its age on close inspection, but it had lasted well enough. She was going to miss this.

The pool was always quiet at 8pm on a Friday, it might be quiet at other times but Maris had no way of knowing. Glen only worked one night a week and she suspected that the other lifeguards would not be as accommodating. She had disliked Glen at first; the pimply youth was genuinely friendly, but he had been prone to lewd comments. Only the expectant look in his eyes suggested that he was merely repeating things he heard elsewhere, his mannerisms painted on like camouflage. He seemed harmless enough though, and the crude phrases had vanished from his lexicon in the last few months.

Maris offered Glen a smile as he waved and clambered down from his seat to start sectioning off a thin lane. She knelt by the poolside to wet the swimming cap, watching a group of old men who were advancing up the pool in a row that forced the other swimmers to make huge detours to avoid them.

As she tugged the cap over her hair an old man broke away from his friends and waved his arms to attract Glen's attention. "It's supposed to be free-swim tonight," he barked.

Glen just grinned down at him. "Yeah I know, I'm only putting this one in." He carried on down the poolside, letting the divider spool out into the water as he went. The old man swelled like a bullfrog, caught between wanting to argue further and needing to keep pace with the lifeguard. In the end, he settled for swimming back to the shallow end, converging on Glen as he knelt to clip the divider into place. Maris dropped into the lane as the old man tugged off his goggles and gestured angrily at Glen.

"It's free swim tonight," he barked again. "It's a poor state of affairs if a lifeguard can't read a damn timetable!"

"Just watch," Glen replied. Maris heard the excitement in his voice and allowed herself a small grin; sometimes it was nice to show off.

She kicked against the wall of the pool and tore through the water like a blade through silk, reaching the opposite wall without needing to draw breath. She spun, kicked, and began the return journey. She switched stroke to butterfly, her entire torso erupting from the water with each kick. Each time she burst through the surface she caught glimpses of the other pool users, shock and amazement showing on their faces. Maris sensed the approaching wall; she rolled, kicked, and began again.

As her body fell into the familiar rhythm her mind drifted, remembering, as she always did, her first swimming lesson. The memory was unavoidable, clinging to her weekly ritual like incense. She remembered her mother's words, the assurance that if she didn't like it, she just had to say the word and they could leave. *Just say the word*, she said, *just say the word and we never have to come back.*

Maris remembered the sense of freedom, the lightness of being, the sheer joy of that first width of the pool. She remembered the shocked delight on the faces of the instructors as she turned back to look for her mother. She remembered the nails digging into her arm as she was dragged from the pool and hauled back to the changing rooms over slippery tiles. Maris' speed increased, her feet churning in fury behind her, but the rush of water against her ears couldn't block out the only words her mother had spoken on the long drive home, the same words she had used when Maris had left home over a decade later. *You are your father's daughter.*

Night had fallen by the time she emerged into the carpark, her hair stiff from the chlorine. She closed her eyes and leaned back against her car, feeling the breeze pick out the damp patches on her skin, trying as she always did to hang on to the sense of freedom she felt in the water. The loose jumper and jeans hung from her like sack-cloth, damp and somehow more confining than the swimming costume. She turned back to the car and unlocked it, pausing as she heard the rapid patter of feet behind her.

"Lady! Hey lady!" It was Glen.

Maris let out a slow breath through her nose, she hated being called 'lady,' like some pampered dog. Then again, she had never told him her name so he didn't have a lot of options. She turned back towards him and saw that that he was carrying her swimsuit, still sodden from the pool; he hadn't paused to wring it out.

"We were just cleaning up," he said brightly. "You, err, you left this in the cubicle."

He held out the soaking costume, drips pattering on the tarmac between them. He stared at her expectantly for a few moments, then seemed to realise how wet the costume was and turned away from her, muttering apologies. Water splashed around his feet as he twisted the material in his hands. At last he turned back to her and Maris took the damp bundle from him, smiling her thanks. Glen tried to open the car door for her but she raised an arm to block him and he flinched, suddenly uncertain. "Well, err," his voice was higher than usual, quavering with nerves. "Have a nice evening." He turned away and hurried back to the building.

Maris watched his retreating back for a moment. Perhaps his friendship group had changed, she wondered, his behaviour still felt borrowed but it was clearly better sourced.

Once back in the car she dumped the costume into the passenger footwell and turned up the volume on the empty CD player, closing her eyes as her ears picked out the crash of the waves beneath the static. She had meant to leave the swimming costume here, another empty vessel left in her wake, but maybe it was just as fitting to take it with her.

She didn't know where she was going yet, and so began a slow circuit of the city. The speakers hissed as the wave song grew, then faded, then grew again as she followed the ring road. At last she turned off onto the main road heading west, the anticipation building in her chest as the waves grew louder. Nothing existed beyond the road, her world now bordered by white lane markings and the orange glow of the streetlights. Beyond, the shapes of trees and buildings blended to one in the darkness, shrouded in sable dustcovers until the world required their use once more.

Sometimes she heard the cry of a seagull issue from the speakers and Maris remembered the old photo album she had found buried in the dust beneath her mother's bed. It had been full of pictures of a girl only few years younger than Maris was now, shy but smiling before a sunlit sea. She had taken it downstairs, wanting to know who the girl was, only realising her mistake when she saw look of horror and rage on her mother's face. Maris remembered the label on the front of the album, 'Dunster 1980' written in a beautiful cursive hand. She froze in her seat, hands tightening on the steering wheel, hardly daring to breathe. Slowing to a stop on the hard shoulder, she switched off the engine and struggled to bring her breathing under control. After several long minutes, Maris started the car and continued her journey west towards the coast. The waves still tugged at her ears but she wasn't listening any more, she didn't need to. She knew where she was going.

Maris parked the car by the side of the road in Blue Anchor Bay. Leaning over the gearstick, she scooped up the swimming costume from the passenger footwell before stepping out onto the pavement. Maris let the still damp material crumple into a ball on the driver's seat before shutting the door. She wasn't sure why she felt the need to do that, it just seemed appropriate.

Advancing to the wall on the other side of the pavement, a waist-high barrier of concrete that marked the edge of this little pocket of civilisation; Maris looked out over the sea. The tide was in, the beach reduced to little more than a thin cordon of sand and pebbles that glistened like black opals beneath the moon. Ignoring the chill wind that blew in from the sea, her mind turned inward. For the first time since she heard the waves whispering from deep in her earphones, Maris wondered what she was doing. She had followed the trail, like a shark scenting blood in the water, every thought and impulse guiding her to this place. There hadn't been space in her head for what should happen next, and now she was here she felt as lost as ever. Her fingers twisted into the wool of her cardigan, hugging it closer as she began to shiver. Her eyes, turned near to black in the light of the moon, stared out over the incoming waves, unseeing. She was vaguely aware of the approaching footsteps, but it was several moments before she realised that they had stopped beside her.

"I knew you'd come one day." The voice was brittle, expectant, and as familiar as the ache from an old injury. Maris froze, her throat tightening. She took a few steadying breaths, then turned to stare into the face of her mother.

The last five years seemed to have taken more than their share from Elizabeth, the skin stretched tight over her cheekbones beneath hair grown lank and tangled. Maris stared, her mind struggling to reconcile this bedraggled figure with the stern matriarch she remembered. Elizabeth stood hunched inside a heavy raincoat that Maris recognised, but which now seemed a couple of sizes too large. Her hands were clenched around the opening of an old shopping bag, holding it tight over her abdomen as though afraid that a hand would reach from the shadows to snatch it. Maris stared at the bag for a moment, unable to look away, the song of the waves growing louder in her ears. At last she tore her eyes away, unfolded her arms and raised her hand to her forehead in greeting.

"Oh why can't you just talk to me? I'm your mother, I know what your voice sounds like." Elizabeth's voice faltered, shame creeping into her eyes as she uttered the old rebuke.

Maris' back stiffened, her jaw setting into a hard line as the last five years evaporated in an instant. She re-crossed her arms and stared into her mother's face, lips clamped together. The silence grew between them, then Elizabeth shook her head and turned to look out over the beach.

"I avoided this place for so long," Elizabeth muttered. "That changed after you left. Seemed to made some sort of sense to be here on your birthday." She looked over her shoulder at

Maris. "You do know it's your birthday? Or had you forgotten?

Maris shifted uncomfortably; she hadn't forgotten, she'd just been preoccupied. In truth she hadn't marked it for two years, but under her mother's eye she began to feel guilty and was relieved when Elizabeth turned her gaze down to the beach.

"I was just over there when I first saw him. Striding out of the waves with nothing to cover himself but the coat, and that was just a grey thing draped over his shoulder." Elizabeth's hands wrung at the bag as she cleared her throat. "Mother had told me about them, the selkie. Old stories don't really prepare you for the real thing. I was only seventeen and he, he was so beautiful." Elizabeth turned and sat back against the wall, and when she looked up there were tears glistening on her cheeks.

Maris kept silent, hardly daring to breathe, her questions held back by the same instinct that had guided her to this place. Her mother had never spoken about Maris' father before.

"In the old stories people steal the coats, force them to stay and marry them. I didn't think I needed to, I thought love was enough. It should have been enough!" Elizabeth's voice shuddered to a halt, her shoulders shaking as she struggled to cuff the tears away with a free hand; the other remained tight around the opening of the bag. Maris stared at her feet, fidgeting, trying to look at anything besides the bag or her mother's tears. She walked to the wall and stared down at the patch of beach her mother had indicated. It looked much like any other, it was hard to imagine the proud creature appearing from the surf.

"All those promises, and then he put the coat back on," Elizabeth whispered, so quiet that Maris could barely hear her. "He put it on and when he changed he didn't know me." Her voice was pure bitterness, her eyes boring into Maris as she spoke. Maris leaned forward on the wall. Some rational part of her mind rebelled against the story but it was a futile gesture; she knew it was true. She felt the question before she uttered it.

"Where?" Her voice was a deep bass croak, rough from years of neglect since the day it was stifled by the laughter of children. "When he left, where did it happen?"

"She speaks," Elizabeth muttered. Maris glared at her, repeating the question with a twitch of her eyebrows.

"Over there," replied Elizabeth, jerking her head towards the beach. "Same place I first saw him, if you must know."

"Show me." Maris wasn't sure why she needed to see it, but the sense of purpose that had vanished when she reached the coast had returned.

Elizabeth didn't seem to have heard her at first, then she pushed past Maris and walked down the stone stairway that jutted out from the wall. Maris followed, sand and pebbles crunching beneath her feet as her mother led her down to the water's edge. The beach looked no more remarkable now than it had from the road.

"It was dark when he left too." Elizabeth stood with her back to the sea, arms drawn tight to her body while her fingers tightened on the bag. "Didn't want to be seen, I suppose, but I saw him. Watched him change and swim away." Elizabeth's voice caught in her throat. She swallowed, then spoke again. "I called out to him, and he looked at me, but he wasn't there. He was just...gone."

Maris stood in in silence, watching the waves as they broke and spread towards their feet before retreating, leaving the sand and pebbles shining like glass. She felt oddly numb. Questions formed and then vanished within her mind, never staying long enough for her to grasp them. Maris could feel her mother watching her, and she found her voice again.

"What am I?" It was all she could think to ask. Elizabeth

lowered her eyes to the bag in her lap, her fingers rubbing at the thin plastic.

"You are your father's daughter. Mother said we should bring you here, that you should be with your own kind, but I couldn't do it." She lifted the bag, pressing it to her chest for a moment before holding it out to Maris who had to restrain herself from snatching it. Gently, she took the bag and untied the handles with unsteady fingers. Inside was a cloak, soft as silk and so black it seemed to drink the light. It was curiously warm, seeming to vibrate to her touch.

"I thought you had to stay near it," Elizabeth sobbed. "So I hid it. I just wanted you to stay." Maris stared at the coat in wonder, mesmerised by the inky folds rippling beneath her fingers. Her chest tightened as a prickling heat began to build behind her eyes. "I'm sorry," Elizabeth whispered.

"I know." Maris' reply was little more than a strangled grunt. A weight seemed to have lifted from her, all fear and confusion fading as she cradled the coat in her arms. They stood in silence for moment, then Maris stepped up to her mother and embraced her, holding her close until the tears subsided. As they moved apart, Maris brushed the hair from Elizabeth's face and looked into her eyes before she spoke. "Will you help me?" Her mother looked as though her tears would begin anew, her eyes darting down to the cloak as though she wished to snatch it back. She sighed, shrinking further into the long coat, then nodded.

Elizabeth held the cloak while Maris' clothes dropped one by one to the sand, then draped the coat about Maris' naked shoulders. She tried to lift her hair free of the collar, only to find that it had merged with the cloak, becoming a single black shroud that ran from crown to ankle. Maris reached up to take her mother's hand and together they walked into the surf until the water lapped about their knees.

"I'm glad I got to see you again," said Elizabeth, her voice high and constrained. She gave Maris' hand a squeeze, which Maris returned before releasing her grip and walking further out until the water reached her waist. The cloak clung tighter to her now, moulding over her skin and binding her legs. She looked back over her shoulder, swaying in the current.

"This isn't goodbye," she called to her mother.

"You don't understand," Elizabeth insisted, fresh tears forming. "When you change you won't know me." Maris shook her head.

"I'll know you," said Maris. "I'm your daughter too."

THE END

WAITING FOR MAREN

Gerlinde De Ryck

SEPTEMBER

OCTOBER (THE FIRST SCAN)

NOVEMBER (TWENTY-WEEK SCAN)

NOVEMBER: THE NAME

a name that sounds nice in Dutch and English

with two syllables

nothing that ends in "y"

or any "ee"- sound actually

jeez

it also can't start with a "G" or "T"

or end with "t", "d" or "de"

Annie?

ends in "ie"

Britt?

ew no

Evelien?

too long

Jo?

too short

How about Maren?

oh! "Maren Machurot"

"De Ryck Machurot" you mean

DECEMBER

CHRISTMAS DAY

JANUARY

HORMONES

PATIENCE (1)

PATIENCE (2)

FEBRUARY

SHOPPING

EVERY DAY

MARCH

ANTENATAL CLASS

APRIL

midwife

DUE DATE = 29 APRIL

NIGHT

4 MAY (EMERGENCY CAESAREAN)

WHEN YOU LOOK INTO DARKNESS

Jess Kershaw

Aliyah watched Earth shrink behind her; a blue-green marble in the vast velvet darkness of space. Her first expedition to the stars.

She was not the first human to punch through the skin of reality into the maddeningly unknowable world of folded-space, questing for an easy way to traverse the universe. She was not the fourth. Or the fifth. Or the twenty-fifth.

But she was going to be the first to succeed. She was going to be the first to live.

"Thirty kleks Ma'am," her captain informed her, tapping his fingers over the console. It glowed blue, like some deep underwater bioluminescence. "I'll leave you to do the last fifteen on your own."

"Sure — uh — " It occurred to her that she didn't know her captain's name; she'd never bothered to learn it.

"Marcus," he said. Aliyah barely heard him. She was considering that if aliens did exist, then they would be wondering about the long-term viability of a species that looked at the hellscape beyond the realm of human understanding, saw their expeditionary crews either die or go completely insane, and thought *okay but what if this time we tried that...*

How marvellous humans were; how *stupid*—

No, she rebuked herself, digging her fingernails sharply into her palm. She couldn't think of past failure; only the success she would have.

She headed through the rust-eaten guts of the ship to her one-woman craft. Her budget hadn't stretched to luxury. *The Sunny Day* was a bucket of shit.

Why did people keep trying? Aliyah was accustomed to keeping up a monologue with herself: there was rarely anyone around willing to talk to her.

She answered her own question:

Maybe greed. The first person to figure out a way to cut tunnels through folded-space — thereby enabling ships to travel millions of lightyears in a day — would be rich beyond their wildest imaginings. You could say it was hubris. Humans, after all, make their gods in their own image and they do not believe that there is anything they cannot do. Perhaps it was desperation: with each year that passed, Earth grew less and less able to support life.

Perhaps it was all those things, and more. But for Aliyah it was simple. She'd thought of something that might work. That had been enough.

She'd said to her colleagues: *I have an idea.*

And the response was uniformly: *oh not again.*

And she said: no, I think I get it. *I think we're scaring them.*

And the response was: *what.*

Aliyah remembered how adamant she had been. No, we're scaring them. We're cutting into their home. *They don't speak our language. They're frightened of us, and they're fighting to defend themselves.*

She nestled herself into the craft, legs cramped at the sides. The hatch closed, displaying a neon readout from her captain:

the Gate will be open in eight kleks.

As she soared forwards — juddering a little within the rickety craft — the captain started up his drill, and split reality open.

The Gate was an indigo, lightning-brocaded throat. It strained at the edges, starlight oscillating and dancing.

And as she approached, she saw that something was twisting and dancing within the Gate; something *alive*. Her heart in her mouth, her hands sweaty, she guided herself as far as she dared, lest the hungry gravity suck her in. She could not be sure that she was not hallucinating. Her mind flew back to the life she had left behind. Her mother was dead; her father had disowned her. She had no children, no friends, no colleagues that could bear her. If she died, she would just be one more foolish human, lost to a venture that — perhaps — none of them should have attempted.

Humans make their gods in their own image, and they are willfully, blindly optimistic; stubborn survivalists who spit in the face of mortality and make their homes on the slopes of active volcanoes, because it is there that the soil is richest. Aliyah realised, with slow and dawning grief, that the only being that would truly miss her was her axolotl, little Queenie. Queenie was in an aquarium in Aliyah's meagre flat. She'd left a reminder, asking her colleagues to feed her — but what if no one did?

Another snap of lightning. Something made of darkness was clawing towards the borders of the Gate. Aliyah's face was wet with tears, and her stomach lurched and twisted. *I'm right. There's something in there. I was right — what in the name of God is it?*

It was too late to undertake any course of action beyond this: stay, with her heart in her mouth and her breath trapped in her throat. The Gate pulsed like a great heart, and from its depth unfolded *something*. It seemed to coalesce from without and within at the same time; the Gate's outline twisted, widening; and were those hands? Yes: vast silver hands grasping the edge of the Gate, yanking it wider. *That isn't possible*, Aliyah thought. But, of course, it was.

She thought of Queenie; her friendly, silly face; the inelegant pink gills that frilled around her neck. Static roared in her ears as her comms flared into frantic life, then died entirely.

And then: something was nudging at her head.

Hello, who are you?

The words just *emerged*, there in her thoughts. Another set of hands — claws? They were amorphous, dancing, defying definition, shifting through shapes so fast that to look at them was to invite madness — joined the first. And a third. And a fourth. Some dissolved into white mist, like a bursting nebula, upon leaving the Gate.

Others *solidified*.

As those *things* left the Gate, entering real-space, they gained a form. A shape. Outlines.

Hello? Who are you? Hello?

Aliyah closed her eyes tight and focused. *Hello, yes, my name is Aliyah —*

What are you?

A friend.

Friend? Friend? Friend?

Yes.

Pain corkscrewed through Aliyah's skull. She closed her eyes; the Gate was a blinding mess of hands/teeth/wings/what. Images flashed through her head: the hard, glittery ground of her Alaskan home. Papers, her papers, all her research, crumbling to ash in her hands. Memories came thick, fast, jumbled and dancing; there was something *in her head*, rooting around. Her father crying; her mother shouting;

white walls; the ashy taste of medication; the sun fading to a pinprick.

It resolved, finally, on a single image: her axolotl, her Queenie, sitting in her tank, along in Aliyah's flat.

Who will feed my Queenie —

All those thoughts, all those memories, all that work, and as this alien entity struggled through the mire of her mind, tossing aside everything that seemed superfluous it unearthed that: the one, core concern. *Who will feed my Queenie.*

What is a Queenie? What is this small thing?

The image again: the axolotl in her green tank, waiting alone.

Yes, she's my friend —

Friend —

It seemed like an eternity, but Aliyah opened her eyes. She tasted blood. She had bitten a good chunk from the inside of her cheek, desperate to keep herself from screaming.

Before her floated a giant, silver axolotl.

"What," she managed. There were pinkish gills, the dusky hue of nebulas. There was a great, affable smile. There were —

Ah, about half a dozen legs. And two tails. The thing opened its mouth, displaying more teeth than could feasibly fit in any creature's maw. And yet there it was.

I suppose, it said, you should call me Queenie. And explain where this wonderful place is.

THE END

INTERCHANGE

Ian Robertson

Malcolm watched through the window as the broad rib cage of Paddington station slid over the train. The carriages were old stock left over from the twenty twenties; their upholstery was faded and their glass windows bore the scars of innumerable bored teenagers trying to scratch their way to relevance. Malcolm's girlfriend Illyia was on her feet before the train shuddered to a halt beside platform two. He looked back at their seats to check they hadn't abandoned some vital bit of luggage but Illyia was already jostling her way forward towards the exit.

"Come on." she called back to him as the doors slid open.

The plastic wheels on Malcolm's bag were noisy against the polished sandstone of the platform and he watched the self-driving suitcase of some lamina-suited businessman whirr past; close to the heels of its master. Malcolm wondered if he could afford a case like it on his student loan, but decided he'd already spent too much on paints and canvas that term.

"Do you remember which pod number we are travelling in?" asked Illyia.

"Erm, it didn't say in the booking confirmation, let's check the boards..."

Ahead of them they saw the black departures screen with "*Earth Schedule*" spelled out above it in large lettering, and scanning down they found their slot: *Barcelona HOP-5046G : 16:15 : On Time : Pod number will be announced at 15:30*.

At the base of the board a large digital clock read *14:43*.

"Ugh, I told you we could have gotten a later train." moaned Illyia "What do you want to do now?"

"Well we need to get though security right? That might take a while."

Ten minutes later they were through security; eyes watering slightly from the probes.

"I don't know about you but I need some wine." declared Illyia, scanning the concourse "I think Vinoras's does a passable Malbec. You want anything to eat?"

"No, but wine sounds good. It will help my nerves!"

"Aw! Don't be nervous! My parents are going to love you and your cute English manners!"

"Oh I hope so, but I'm more nervous about the teleportation right now to be honest..."

"Ah of course, this is your first hop! Don't worry there's nothing to it, but still, let's get you some wine."

They seated themselves in the Vinora's serving area: a cluster of screen-topped tables separated from the thoroughfare by a long metal planter full of almost convincing plants. A few swipes and taps on the digital surface and their drinks arrived through a pneumatic tube that ran up from beneath the table. Each measure of wine came in a capped pseudo-glass tumbler to ensure against spillage but a small rivulet of wine escaped from Malcolm's as he unscrewed the top.

"They have these tube things everywhere in London now," said Illyia "I wonder if we'll get them up in Brum."

"God I hope not, what's wrong with having your drink brought to you by a robot? I reckon it's just a gimmick, won't catch on."

There is something bleak about this place. Malcolm stared up with vacant curiosity at the holographic adverts playing down from the wide arched roof of the terminal. A new ad offering changes in skin pigmentation was playing, and to underscore all the absurd skin colours you could choose between a giant purple face emerged from the ceiling, grinning down from the holographic heavens in three hideous dimensions. A stray pigeon had gotten into the atrium somehow and Malcolm watched as it swooped wildly, trying to dodge that giant mouth of grinning white teeth. Next, the poor bird found itself caught amongst violent explosions of light as the holo-ceiling began projecting a vibrant firework display; an advert for 'Release™' orgasm enhancement pills.

"Maybe we should try those?" said Illyia, poking Malcolm's leg with her foot.

"Hmm?" He replied, losing track of the panicked pigeon somewhere behind the logo.

"I'm joking Romeo, we don't need to try any of those!"

Malcolm smiled as Illyia's hand squeezed his knee under the table. He reached for it, interlocking their fingers and feeling her knuckles grip in return. He watched her lips purse against the rim of her wine glass and realised he hadn't looked at her anywhere near enough that day. They had both been so caught up in getting from place to place to place that he'd failed to see her properly, but there she was, even more stunning than usual. *Was her hair a darker shade of black? Her lipstick a deeper shade of red? Her smile more confident somehow?* Malcolm wondered all of this and yet failed to verbalise the questions. Soon he was distracted again: through the plastic plants he saw a queue forming at the base of the ramp leading up to pod four.

"I wonder if that will be the pod they put us in?" said Malcolm, nodding towards it. *They could at least make these things look sleeker...* he thought, suspicious of all the chromium tubing and oddly shaped boxes that erupted from the sides of the spherical transport pod. Each bit presumably had some vital purpose and Malcolm really hoped all of them worked reliably. The queuing travellers looked relaxed though and none of them seemed alarmed by the misty steam sinking out of several vents at the bottom of the vessel.

"Still nervous?" Asked Illyia.

"Not really," He said, lying both to her and himself. "More curious really. How's your wine?"

"Overpriced but passable. Yours?"

"Same."

Malcolm watched a man in a high-vis jacket appear from the sphere and step onto the ramp. He gave a thumbs-up sign to someone below and a barrier was lowered. The queue shuffled forward.

"We'll get a carafe of proper Tempranillo in Barcelona as soon as we get out of the station. It will be siesta still, but some places serve early."

"Yeah? Can we sit out in the gothic quarter with some tapas maybe?"

"If you like, but Mama will be force feeding you everything Spanish tonight, so remember to save room!"

Smiling past Illyia Malcolm watched the queue behind her slowly diminish as each traveller disappeared inside the sphere, luggage following closely behind them. A man climbed the ramp with a small a girl perched on his shoulders, her blonde hair was tied into two pigtails and she clutched a green furry toy; it was some cuddly monster that Malcolm couldn't quite recognise. The pair of them approached the entrance to the pod and he wondered if the scene would make a good painting. *Innocence stepping into the unknown...* The girl began to wave her toy excitedly.

"Oh no!" said Malcolm

"What?"

"A little girl has lost her toy!"

"What little girl? What?"

"Over there on that ramp." The noise of wailing tears began to reach them, her wet sobs sounding eerie amongst the cold echoes of the atrium. "Oh, no it's ok, someone's gone to get it for her..."

Malcolm kept watching as the toy was returned to its distraught owner and the last of the passengers trooped inside the sphere. The man in the high-vis jacket reappeared and, standing outside the doorway, pressed a series of buttons. First the inner door snapped closed — solid grey metal emblazoned with a union jack — then the outer door slid shut — no insignia on it except a black number 4. As the man walked downwards the ramp began to retract behind him. The sphere stood alone in empty space and beneath it hydraulics shuddered into life; a concertina of metal began to lift the pod slightly, then lowered it slightly more. It all looked like a fairground ride that was about to bounce and spin for simple giddying thrills.

"They're off" Commented Malcolm, glancing back at the departures board... "Do you know why the pod has to move up and down like that?"

"I heard it is something to do with small changes in gravity" said Illyia "movements of magma inside the earth or something, so they have to adjust things a little each time."

"What if the magma moved suddenly? Could it throw you into mid-air by accident?"

"Don't be silly, that's what planes are for!"

"Sure, but I quite like planes... Oh look! See something's gone wrong! The ramp is going back... Oh god and there's smoke coming out of the top bit!"

Illyia glanced over her shoulder just as the sphere's outer doors slid open. The inner doors looked the same as they had a moment ago, except the Union Jack had gone, replaced by a red circle on a white oblong. This Japanese flag then split apart as the inner doors opened too.

"No I think that's normal..." said Illyia.

"Was that it?" Malcolm saw calm faces emerge from the pod. *Are they different from the faces that walked in?* There was no sign of blonde pigtails or a green toy. *Is that little girl really in Japan now? Walking out of a pod on the other side of the world?* Malcolm experienced a strange, directionless, vertigo... he was sitting in a terminal full of ramps and doorways that could lead anywhere, and once you stepped through and the man pressed the buttons behind you... who even knew what space you were in then? "I was expecting a noise or a flash of light or something." He said.

"Nope, it's all just a big anti-climax. Want another drink?"

"Erm no, our pod number is up, we should go."

"Oh okay." They both stood to leave "Oh but we have to put our wine glasses back in the tube I think, otherwise they bill us for them."

"Oh really? Sure."

Following Illyia's example Malcolm screwed the lid back on his glass and placed it in the hatchway of the tube. He closed the lid and pressed the button.

Nothing happened.

"It's not going..."

"Press the button!"

"I tried that."

"So try it again, or did you break it with your man fingers?"

"It's not my fault it's broken!" said Malcolm, and he began mashing the button with a sudden anger.

"Oh I see the problem." Illyia reached forward, opened the tube door, and then closed it again. "There, try now."

This time the glass disappeared without incident and Malcolm felt a heady mixture of humiliation and relief. "Welcome to the future babe!" said Illyia grinning.

Malcolm looked at her slowly and summoned a weak smile as they gathered their luggage. "Oh brave new world that hath such people in it." he mumbled.

"Huh? What are you saying Englishman?"

"I don't know, it's a quote from somewhere... I forget where," said Malcolm shrugging. Before Illyia could break his gaze to continue their journey he reached for her hand, pulled her towards him and planted his lips on hers. Behind him his suitcase toppled slowly, but he let it fall, sliding his hands around his partner instead. He hugged her tightly, feeling her warmth along the length of his body, someone to cling to in a madly swirling universe, the only point in space that mattered.

The departure board directed them to pod eight. It wasn't far along the concourse and they had plenty of time; Illyia held Malcolm's hand as they joined the queue that had already formed at the base of their ramp. She smiled at him quietly as they stood motionless in this rank of strangers. Malcolm smiled back trying not to think about the metal doors ahead, or the steam that emerged from beneath them, or even the wine he had just drunk, as it seemed to be sitting strangely inside him. He reminded himself that people had been doing this for over a decade now, and the web-sites and trust-sites all reassured him that, unlike air-travel, no one had ever been killed or injured by *commercial* teleportation... Although that wasn't the same as saying no one *could* ever be killed by commercial teleportation was it? Despite his unanswered question, Malcolm hadn't searched for information about *experimental* teleportation accidents. He was too broke to afford plane tickets anyway.

The doors of pod eight slid open and another high-vis man appeared. Or perhaps it was the same man from pod four who'd teleported over? Who even knows these days. The queue of people and luggage began to inch towards the pod entrance like toothpaste being squeezed up a tube. Malcolm focused on the feel of Illyia's fingers squeezing against his and soon their feet were climbing the checker-plated metal ramp as the man held out the ticket scanning machine, acknowledging each passenger with a disinterested smile as the machine bleeped at them and flashed green.

As they stepped through the door and into the pod Malcolm let out an odd laugh.

"What's funny?" Asked Illyia.

"Look, they stole your line!"

On the other side of the sphere, past milling passengers and concentric curved benches, a holo-window was displaying three dimensional panoramas of various different pod-destinations, in front of which pulsed the words: "*Welcome to the future*" in free-floating letters.

"Here we go" said Illyia, as the last of the passengers filed in "Five minutes until Tapas!"

Malcolm closed his eyes as the doors slid inwards towards each other. There were no *real* windows to look out of anyway. In the intraocular darkness it was easier to focus on the calming suction of his lungs and the feeling of Illyia's hand pressed against his slightly sweaty palm. The pod shuddered gently as it adjusted position the thought occurred to Malcolm that in that moment he really had no idea where he was. With his eyes closed he could still hear murmuring of machinery and passengers around him, he could still feel Illyia in one hand and his suitcase in the other, but were they still in London or already in Barcelona? Was he still inside the pod even? Would his body be the same body when he opened his eyes again?

Back in Paddington station the stray pigeon saw an expanse of clear blue sky in the background of a fruit juice advert. The bird forced its last remaining energy into its wings and made a break for freedom. It swooped downwards to dodge a looming glass full of gravity defying liquid, then swerved from side to side to evade a sudden downpour of tumbling mangos, peaches, and pineapples, and yet doggedly it climbed higher and higher with each swoop and turn. Finally the pigeon was past all holographic obstacles and flying in infinite blue space, the terrors of the interchange terminal diminishing behind it. Free at last, it broke its neck colliding with the ceiling.

THE END

THE BAR

Abigail B. Vint

"Guess you're wondering why I'd come into a place like this and order a coffee?" A slender older man took a sip of the steamy drink in front of him, catching the bartender's eye.

"Not my place to judge," said the bartender, softly shaking his head and turning his attention towards the empty glasses along the bartop.

The man nodded and cleared his throat before he spoke.

"It's just that, well, I don't frequent pubs much anymore on account of, well..." The man looked side to side to see if anyone else in the bustling place was listening in.

When he turned back, the bartender had moved a bit closer and stood right in front of him. The patron's voice faded away along with the courage to continuing his story.

The bartender rescued him.

"We get lots of different folk in here, for lots of different reasons. You wouldn't be the first guy who I've slid a cup of coffee to across the bar."

The bartender smiled and picked up a clean wine glass to start polishing.

The man exhaled and took another sip of coffee. Gulp swallowed, he spoke again. "Name's Bart. Bart McCauley."

"Ralph. It's just Ralph," the bartender replied.

"Nice to meet you, Ralph."

"You too," Ralph said, setting down the first glass and picking up another from the shelf.

Bart looked past Ralph to see a woman, her deep red hair was tied up in a messy bun, her clothes looked a bit over-sized and her face, scrunched up, eyebrows almost meeting.

The loud speaker boomed.

"Mrs. Johnson, your table is ready."

The redhead at the end of the bar popped open her droopy eyes and stared for a few seconds before stepping down off her bar stool.

She said nothing to Ralph, just gave him a nod, and turned to walk away from the bar and towards the lighted area.

"Hmm," said Bart, shaking his head and wrapping his hand around the mug while the other stayed clasped, firm, on the handle. "She must have been here awhile," Bart looked at his watch. "Don't suppose you know how long?"

Ralph chuckled as he watched the redhead leave his bar area.

"Nope, not a clue. That's just the way it goes."

Bart shifted in his bar stool, catching a whiff of the fresh air blowing in before taking another sip.

"How long have we been waiting?" a tall, dark-haired woman barked at the young man beside her.

He was wearing an army uniform, fairly new and not many stripes. Only a keen eye would have noticed the splotch of blood on the left chest of his jacket. Her booming voice made him lean away from her, his shoulders tensing, his stare, straight ahead.

"I'm not sure, ma'am. I'm having trouble keeping track of

time in here," he turned back to his soda water and the woman pulled back a bit, sensing she was invading his space.

"Don't worry about it. I'm being just being impatient." When she got no reply, she added. "Sorry, didn't mean to take it out on you."

The soldier's shoulders relaxed and he took a deep breath, in and out. He straightened up on his stool and took a big slurp from the straw he'd requested in his drink.

"It's just, I'm not very good at just sitting around, waiting for someone to arrive or something to happen. I'm a very busy person, or, at least I was until recently..." She turned away from the soldier, who was simply staring straight ahead, and caught a glimpse of her own puzzled face in the mirror behind the bar.

She was about to comment on the grey hair she saw glinting in the light when Ralph suddenly appeared in front of her reflection.

"Everything alright over here?"

The soldier nodded. "Yes, sir. The water is great, sir. Thank you, sir."

"You can just call me Ralph, soldier, no lines of command in here."

"OK, Ralph, sir—oh! Shit I did it again, sorry sir. I mean, sorry Ralph."

Ralph laughed and pulled the soda jet towards the almost empty cup with a straw.

"Lemme refill you, kid. I think you may be here for a bit."

The soldier didn't try to speak this time and just nodded enthusiastically as his face turned red.

The woman beside the soldier took her chance. "Well, I have a question, Mr... Mr. Ralph, you said?"

"It's just Ralph," he replied to the woman, who was now leaning forward towards him, as if trying to block out all others in his sight.

"Jane Stemple," the woman thrust her almost opaque white hand out and grasped Ralph's with a strong, firm grip. "I feel like I've been waiting here for some time and—" She stopped, mid-thought. "So, you're just Ralph, then? No surname?"

"Nope, it's just Ralph. I have a middle name but I don't bother with it," he said.

"Right, I see. Though I do think if your mother took the time to give you a first and middle name it's only—" Jane stopped as Ralph turned from her.

"Oh wait! Ok ,yes, I'm sorry, me and my big mouth."

Ralph turned back around this time with silver bill plates in his hand.

"Just doing a bit of reorganizing," he held them up to show her. "Like to move things around a bit, keep it interesting."

Jane opened her mouth as if she was going to speak again but then closed it, muttering to herself.

Ralph set the plates down and moved closer to Jane.

"You'll have to speak up if you want me to hear you, ma'am," Ralph shook his head slightly, glancing quickly to see if Jane noticed his gesture.

Jane looked up, shocked.

"Oh it's just that... I'm just wondering, what is the hold up with my table?"

Ralph raised his hands. "I don't have anything to do with what comes next," he said. "You'll just have to wait until they call you, like everyone else."

She let out a curt sigh. "You know, I actually usually have quite a lot on my schedule. I can't imagine my PA would have accounted for all of this waiting around. I'm sure there's somewhere I ought to be right now."

Ralph started to walk away from her, assuming she didn't want any more to drink.

"You'll just have to wait until they call you, ma'am. In the meantime, maybe you could get to know this young lad beside you here. He's looking a little anxious himself."

She turned to the soldier, noting the way his brown hair fell into his eyes. *He needs a haircut*, she thought. *And maybe a bit of confidence.* Something about him made her heart rate slow and her shoulders relax.

"I see you like soda water," she said. "Not a drinker then?" She raised her almost empty gin and tonic to clarify what kind of drinking she was referring to. The soldier said nothing and began counting the number of bottles behind the bar. "Has that always been your drink of choice or are you..."

Her voice blended into the blanket of sound hovering over the patrons, a jukebox off in the distance playing some popular 60s tune, and Ralph disappeared from her view. He walked back to the other end of the bar, grabbed another glass and started polishing.

An elderly couple entered, taking their time to settle into their seats at the small table in the corner. Neither of them really seemed to fit in the bar but they didn't seem to be making a fuss about why they were there.

"I guess they'll call us," the man said.

The woman shouted back, "YOU SAY THEY'RE DELIRIOUS?"

The man rolled his eyes and spoke louder.

"I said they'll CALL US." He spoke slowly and got as close to her left ear as possible.

The woman nodded her head as she sat down. Her husband, surprisingly out of breath from their short walk, waited until she was fully seated until lowering himself down into the bucket chair.

Ralph was at their table before they'd finished this slow sitting routine.

"Welcome to The Bridge. What can I get for you?"

The woman of the pair jumped and let out a small gasp, clenching her blue cold hands into fists and lifting them closer towards her chest. The man slowly reached out and lowered the tight hands down into her lap. "You're alright, pet, you're alright." The woman smiled and her body sank, releasing back into the chair.

Ralph stood patiently by their table, not moving, not fussing and not, really, helping.

"Oh, good day Mr..." the man looked closely at Ralph's nametag. "Mr. Ralph."

Ralph jumped in. "You can just call me Ralph."

The old man chuckled and corrected himself.

"Ah, yes, lovely. Good day, Ralph."

He squinted his eyes looking past Ralph towards the bar to see if he could find something of interest.

"I think I'd really just like a quality whiskey. Do you have any of the good stuff? Say, over 10 years old, single malt?"

"We can certainly arrange that, sir."

The old man's surprise showed he hadn't been treated like a proper bar guest in a long time.

"Well, that will do me just fine, then. Your finest whiskey."

Ralph leaned in closer and got right close into her ear before he spoke in a solid volume. "And for you, madam?"

The old woman took her chances, seeing as her husband was able to get exactly what he wanted.

"Can you make a Twinkle, double? It's a drink I used to have many moons ago. It would be lovely to have a sip of that." Her face turned upwards, lost in a memory of time past.

She turned to Ralph, eager and hopeful, to which he replied a small nod.

"An aged single malt whiskey and a Twinkle. I like it when my clients have particular tastes."

Ralph turned back around to the bar, leaving the elderly couple staring into each others eyes, mouths turned up slightly into soft smiles, their bodies melting into the plush chairs.

He had only just gotten back around behind the bar, when he noticed a new face had joined his crew.

A young woman, face blotchy red, her hair tangled and clothes, plain and layered.

"I think I'm supposed to wait here. I think this is where we're supposed to meet." Her hands lay flat on the bartop, eyes down, looking at the vacant space between her fingers. She did not appear to notice Jane, the soldier or Bart.

"You're in the right place," Ralph said, wiping the bartop where her gaze was fixed. The sight of his hand and cloth brought her eyes up to meet his. "You stay right here and when it's your time, they'll call you."

"Thank you," she breathed out. "Thank you, I would like to just wait. Just wait right here."

The vacant stare came back, hands still resting as though bookends to something special in the middle of the bartop.

"Let me get you something," Ralph tried to engage again. "You may be here for awhile," he said, placing his hands on top of hers and leaning in towards her. It wasn't very often he used the healing power of touch. Still amazed him when someone did take to his approach.

"Just a Coke. A Coke, please," she pulled her hands out from under Ralph's and her stare met his. "With ice. My husband used to make it with ice, a whole glassful of ice." A small smile spread across her face and she brought her clasped hands towards her lips, closing her eyes.

"We've got lots of ice. One Coke filled with ice."

He made the young woman's order, sliding the requested drink in front of her.

"This one's on Ralph" he said. "That's me, Ralph the

bartender."

Getting drinks for customers wasn't always encouraged, but if there was one thing Ralph learned over the years, it was that his job was to make people happy. To get them in the right, relaxed headspace and ready to head on. He'd pretty much do anything he thought that would get the person closer to their table. Anything to get him closer to the end of his shift.

The woman looked up, a healthier peach replaced the red in her cheeks.

"Thank you, Ralph, the bartender," she whispered without meaning to be quiet. "I'm Ella. Ella with the Coke in ice."

"Well, Ella, it looks like you're all set for now. Just hang tight here until they call you."

Ella took a long drink, her lips disappearing behind the ice cubes. Ralph busied himself behind the bar, looking for that vintage whiskey he had promised.

"Looks like you might need a refill there," Ralph said, grabbing the coffee pot and heading towards Bart.

Bart pushed his coffee mug towards Ralph.

"Never say no to another round," Bart said, and winced a bit at his joke. "That was part of my problem in the first place," he said.

"It's always time for another round of coffee," Ralph said.

"Guessing you've had your fair share of coffee over the years. How long have you worked here anyway?"

Ralph didn't often get this question. Most people were preoccupied with their own wait, they never really put any thought towards those providing the service.

"It's hard to say," Ralph replied, returning the coffee jug to its place in the machine and turning his attention towards the whiskey bottles on the bar. "Depends who you ask as well."

"Not sure I've seen anyone else here around to ask. For all I know, you could be the owner of this joint."

Ralph laughed and turned away and Bart kept his eyes on him, waiting to see if he would reveal anything. Ralph simply approached the back of the bar, pouring a measure of the nicest malt whiskey they had in the place, for the elderly patron, and was now searching for the champagne to get started on a Twinkle.

"I'm certainly here a lot," Ralph replied, distracted by his search. "But, that's what they pay me the big bucks for."

Bart chuckled and his head turned quickly towards the jingle bell of the door. A group of men were piling in, single file, all wearing workmen's hats and tar dirty overalls. No one else in the bar seemed to notice them enter, too focused on themselves.

"I can't imagine how difficult that must have been for you, growing up without your mother," Jane had turned to face the soldier beside her, and had all but forgotten the hurry she was in.

"Yeah," the soldier replied. "I guess it was," rolling his fingers around his cold soda water. "I guess I didn't know what I was missing but there was always a little part of me that felt, unfinished."

He turned to face Jane, who had leaned closer towards him along the bar.

"I'm sure your mother would want to complete that puzzle for you. To make sure you knew just how loved you were," Jane voice grew more urgent as she spoke. "To make you whole."

She was gripping the soldier's arm now, and Ralph turned just in time to see the intensity between them.

"We're all made up of different puzzle pieces," said Ralph.

"Sometimes we lose a few along the way but we can't move forward until we find a way to make it all fit back together again."

Both Jane and the soldier looked up at Ralph, startled by his sudden presence.

"Yes," Jane said, "Of course. Fitting all the pieces back together."

She turned to the soldier.

"What did you say your name was?"

"Fields. Derek Fields."

Jane gasped and involuntarily grabbed at her stomach. She pursed her lips into a smile, waiting a few deep long breaths before speaking.

"Well, I'm sure you'll find her," she said, slurping the last of her drink. "She'd be lucky to be in my seat, having a drink with you, listening to you talk about all of your achievements."

Jane pulled back, wrapping her arms around herself and turning to face the back of the bar, closing her eyes tightly as two small tears rolled down her cheeks.

Ella had been staring at the ice cubes in the bottom of her Coke long enough not to realise quite how long it had been. She twirled the straw around the cubes and took a look around the place.

The bar was brighter than others she'd been in - something about the way the light glowed. The blue fluorescent rays beaming from under the bar shelves. About a dozen standing lights were littered around the place, tall like trees, she thought, towering over all of the guests. The music seemed to change from early 1920s right up to modern rock. An interesting mix, she thought, possibly considering the crowd was diverse in age. As she turned to look one by one to the individuals in the bar, she noticed they all looked perfectly lit, like a set designer had come in and made sure everyone was showing their best side.

She couldn't remember the last time she was at a bar and everyone looked so good. She laughed to herself, remembering she had met her husband Ross in a bar. Young and full of life, they'd both been. They managed to carry on a conversation amid the strobing lights and the screeching voices. That was such a long time ago, she thought. So much longer than it should feel, she thought. Puzzled, she placed both her hands on the bar to ground herself. Ella pinched her arm, just to make sure she wasn't dreaming. She was still sat at the bar. At this bright lit bar. She had been so wrapped in her own thoughts she hadn't even heard the bell on the door of jingle as someone new entered the bar.

"Ella, you waited."

She looked up. It was Ross. She felt her heart try to burst outside of her chest and took a few seconds before she flung her arms around his neck.

"You're here. You're finally here." She nestled her face into his broad shoulder, taking in the smell of his cologne.

The voice over the loudspeaker came on.

"Mr and Mrs Sheraton, your table is ready."

Ella stood up and followed Ross out. She was almost out of the bar before she turned back to catch Ralph's eye.

"Thanks for the Coke, Ralph the bartender," she said. Ralph gave her a nod and Ella turned away, staying close behind Ross as they left.

"There doesn't really seem to be any order people get called. Some must get pretty frustrated?" Bart had just returned from the toilet and was hopping back up on his barstool. Ralph was going for refill number six in the coffee cup.

"Yeah, people can be a bit impatient but part of my job is to keep them calm, make sure they're relaxed, focussed on what they need to be so their table is called."

Bart looked puzzled.

"You need to focus to get your table?"

"Sometimes. It all really depends if they've got the appropriate spot for you on the other side. I find if people are fixated on why they are still here, their table is never likely to be called."

Bart touched his lips tentatively on the edge of his mug. The steam appeared to be giving the right temperature. He pulled back quickly and set the mug down.

"I'll just give that a minute."

"That's what I like to hear," Ralph said as he started to walk towards the other end of the bar to serve the latest arrival. "A bit of patience."

"I'm surprised a classy lady like yourself would be here in a place like this all by yourself." Derek attempted to turn the conversation toward Jane, who had been peppering him with questions for the last ten minutes.

Jane laughed and shook her head.

"Oh well, I think that's very sweet of you to say but I'm quite content on my own. Always been a bit busy for other people," she turned to see Derek's expression, unsure she was giving the impression she wanted.

"Ah yeah, I like to be by myself too. That's why the army was a bit tough for me, close quarters and all. But my Aunt Marg said it was the best for me."

Jane went white.

"Marg Walken?"

Derek's face look confused.

"Well, yeah, but how do you know my Aunt's name?"

Jane could not move but she took a large inhale before she spoke.

"She used to be my babysitter," Jane said. "She was a wonderful woman. I remember even as a young 7 or 8 year old how much she wanted children."

Derek was staring now, intense.

"It wasn't until I was in my teens that I found out she couldn't have any of her own. So when I..."

Jane stopped. She could feel her heart beating fast. It was a moment she had been waiting for all her life and she wanted to get it right.

"When I had my own son, very young, far too young, she took me in. I lived with her and her husband, George, for those first few years. With her, and my son. We lived in a big farmhouse with a bright red door - "

Derek jumped in.

"...and a blue picket fence. It wrapped all the way around the front of our house."

Jane exhaled again and took hold of Derek's hands.

"Yes, Derek, yes we did. We all did together.

Derek's mouth hung open for a few seconds. "Aunt Marg took me in after my mom couldn't care for me. I was only..."

"Three years old," Jane finished his sentence.

Derek's eyes widened. Neither of them spoke. They just stared at each other. Derek leaned in towards Jane and she squeezed tightly and brought her cheeks to his knuckles, pressing her face lightly into the young soldier's hands. A small tear trickled down her face and Derek's eyes filled with water, threatening to spill out.

Derek was about to speak when the loud speaker came on.

"Jane and Derek, your table is ready for you now."

Without one word passing between them, both Jane and Derek stood up and headed towards the door. Right before they reached the bright exit, she gently placed her left arm around him, guiding him through the well lit doorway.

The old man had been sipping away at his drink, trying to make it last.

"I'm not sure how long we'll be here, pet," he said. "But I can tell you, this whiskey is sure making the wait a bit easier."

His wife was lost in the taste of her Twinkle. She didn't reply initially, but before taking another sip, she bellowed, "HOPE YOUR DRINK IS WORKING OUT OK, LOVE."

The old man winced at her booming voice but said nothing.

He heard the sound of a slurp and looked over to see his wife, tipping the martini glass almost upside down to finish off the drink. He smiled remembering how much he reminded her of the first night they met. He was on leave from the front lines and went in search of some drink and excitement when he found the place. A small drinking hole down a windy alley, a few letters on the sign fallen down, most likely from the regular bombing in the area. He opened the door and that's when he was stopped in his tracks. Frozen and staring at the most beautiful girl he'd ever seen. His friends piled in after him, pushing around him to get to the bar, except for Gilly, who paused and grabbed at his arm.

"C'mon, mate, what are you waiting for? Let's get a pint in," Gilly said.

"I'm going to marry that girl," he said and Gilly burst into laughter.

"That one behind the bar? You're punching above your weight, mate," Gilly said and wandered off, shaking his head as he went.

Turned out the old man was right, he did marry her. Unlike the rest of the soldiers, who had been leering and vulgar, he sat the bar that whole night, nursing a couple single malt whiskeys and keeping her company.

"I'd like to buy you a drink," he said, after the second hour of simply rolling the ice cubes around a short glass. She scoffed.

"Well, I'd love to sit down and have one, but who's going to be pouring if I do that?" she said, addressing the next man in uniform and starting to pull his pint.

"I could help you with that too," he said.

She protested. "Nah, you men are working hard enough, fighting out there on the front lines. Least I can do is pull these pints until my brother gets back," her expression changed at the mention of her brother, who, the old man found out later, owned the bar and was flying with the air force.

"Tell you what, soldier, when this war is over and you're still looking to take me for a drink, you come back here and we'll head over to my favourite cocktail bar," she said, the smile reappearing.

As he had left that night, she shouted out to him "Twinkle."

He looked at her puzzled.

She shook her head and shouted again. "That cocktail you're going to buy me. Don't forget," she wagged her finger, flashed him another smile and turned back towards the taps to pull some more pints.

Forget he did not. And, looking at her now, enjoying the one of her favourite drinks, he saw her just as he had all those years ago.

"You always did like a Twinkle," he said, quietly, more to himself. He was taken aback when she turned and said softly, "You were the first boy to ever buy me one. Loved them even more since then."

The old man's eyes welled up and he raised his glass

towards her. Just as he swallowed down his last tiny sip, the intercom man's voice filled the bar again.

"Mr. and Mrs. Banks, your table is ready for you."

He tried to keep the tears tucked away behind his eyes. He looked over at his wife who took one last long slurp of her bubbly concoction before standing slowly to make a move.

"Let's go, pet. They've called us."

"You sure do have a way with people," Bart said to Ralph as they watched the woman and her son walk out of the bar.

"Thanks. I do try," Ralph said, leaning against the bar and turning towards Bart.

"It just seems like a lot of work, especially for a guy who's paid to serve drinks."

"I like that part of my job," Ralph said. "I enjoy helping people, bringing them comfort, whether that's in a drink or a conversation. Some people need more healing than others, so my level of attention can vary, depending on the case."

The old couple slowly approached the bar and the old man lifted his hand towards Ralph.

"Thank you, sir, you're a bit of a miracle worker. That drink did wonders. I say, you're an angel among men," he said, giving a wave and headed towards the lit exit, his wife leading the way.

And there it was, Ralph thought. Those five little letters.

Ralph knew it wouldn't be long now, an appreciative smile appearing on his face.

He was so caught up in watching what would be his final customer walk out the door, he hadn't noticed Bart had appeared behind the bar alongside him.

"Hey Ralph, looks like your shift is finishing. I'll have to finish that last cup of coffee later," Bart said as he placed a firm hand on Ralph's shoulder.

"So, it was you," his voice faraway, Ralph still hadn't moved from his spot. "I knew this day was coming but I just didn't have..." his voice trailed off, his eyes wide staring over at Bart's knowing expression.

"Well, they didn't tell me much either. Just to wait for the word and then start doing your work," Bart pointed down at his apron. "I can take that from you now."

Ralph turned to the Bart, his eyes a bit wet and nodded. He fumbled a bit with his bar apron, his hands shaking as he tried to remove it, only just realising it had never come off before. He kept his focus on the knot, tried not to look around at the people still left that were no longer his responsibility. Trying not to think too hard about what came next or that, ultimately, even he didn't know where he was headed.

"Right, ok..." Ralph placed the apron on the bar. "Lemme catch you up to speed on who's still here."

Bart raised his right hand in protest.

"Not necessary, my friend, I've been keeping an eye out."

Ralph nodded, still stunned at the prospect of leaving the bar and looked around to see if there was something he should do.

Quickly placing the glasses in the dishwasher, he looked around to collect any personal items.

But there was nothing there behind the bar that Ralph needed. He swiped his hands together, flicking away any excess water from the dishes, and turned to shake Bart's hand.

"Well, I guess that's me, then," Ralph said. "I'll be seeing you."

He looked towards the exit, hesitated before starting towards the door. Bart nodded in encouragement.

"I think I've got it from here," Bart said.

Ralph turned his back on the bar, straightening his back,

walking steady but slow.

Just before he reached the exit, Bart called out, "Any advice?"

Ralph smiled and looked down at his feet, thinking about what exactly it had been that he had done over all these years.

"Just listen, without judgement, keep it light, tell a joke or two," he said. "And always make sure drinks are filled, especially those with the coffee cups."

Bart laughed and gave Ralph a wave, turning to address the new woman who had just joined climbed up on a barstool.

Ralph heard Bart engage. "What can I get you today? A hot drink or something stronger?"

"Oh, well, I'm just waiting for someone so I think I'll just take a water for now. I'm not sure when..."

Their voices melted into the crowd noises. And so Ralph made his way, away from the brightness of the bar and into the light outside.

THE END

THE UNDERNEATH

Alex Ware

Only five days had passed. She wondered how she... how anyone... could survive like this.

Joanne stood within a small shelter on the outskirts of a slovenly metropolis, known as the Underneath. She'd at least had the fortune to be assigned to District 3 — slovenly but still pretty safe. An elderly neighbour of hers remembered the days when District 3 was a lively town with its own identity, like the other districts. However, all individuality had been lost to the flowing tides of history. Now they were just holding bays for the damned, numbered sequentially. At least there was running water, sanitation, primitive technology. Everything you needed to start a happy, healthy new life, as she'd been told upon arrival.

She'd returned to the arrivals station every day, as a small part of her hoped that Michael might come down to save her from this wretched place. On some days, she expected that her implants would re-activate, or that this had all been a nightmare she'd eventually wake up from. Down here in the Underneath, it felt as though everyone were waiting for retribution in one form or another.

Presently, she was waiting alone. New arrivals appeared

on a daily basis. Each time they were handed a small, poorly-written booklet explaining the new status quo, and she imagined the arrivals feeling the sadness of loss and acceptance washing over them as they thumbed numbly through its pages in their new living quarters.

The arrivals station was clearly some repurposed abandoned bus station, reeking of damp brickwork and fear, lined with benches, and desks supporting numerous scattered piles of blank forms. Just like her, it watched and waited for something.

A small rodent scurried from a pile of trash in the corner and fled into the dark, stagnant night, startling Joanne out of her trance. Calming herself down, her eyes were drawn to an indecorous, slightly torn arrivals poster. In imposing block letters, it read:

WELCOME TO DISTRICT 3!

Beneath this, the poster continued:

"We hope you'll find everything you need to start a happy, healthy new life. For full information on your new home, please read the instruction booklet issued by your arrivals officer. Your implants will have been deactivated upon arrival. Please follow your designated officer to your new quarters. After your first week, you will undergo a series of aptitude tests which will help assign you to a career path. For your safety and security, please remain within the confines of the Underneath until granted clearance to the outer world."

Sighing, she picked up a booklet on the side and read through it again, still finding it somewhat lacking in information. As it detailed, the districts served as rehabilitation centres for those who had lost their place in the Kingdom, up above. In that artificial paradise, a vast servile network of mechanical implants and operatives served the citizens' every need. Knowledge could be acquired in an instant. The flesh became immortal and would begin to close as soon as it was cleaved, repair as soon as it was bruised.

Eternal life had been assured. Since the population could not die off, the citizens were limited by strict rules on reproduction. Unfortunately; her falling pregnant had been in violation of those rules.

In the Underneath, there was no such network of machinery and implants. Exiled citizens at least found themselves in a functional, contained environment, to help them readjust to the minutiae of everyday life.

Joanne listlessly discarded the booklet, she'd already come to remember what these 'minutiae' were. They were the daily sufferings of hunger and pain, the toils of fatigue, the restless aches of boredom, sadness, loss. She winced in pain and clutched her shoulder, which had been roughed up by the guards upon her exile.

Truth be told, it wasn't the nature of suffering itself which so encumbered her. It was the sheer RELENTLESSNESS of it. Joanne was consigned helplessly to the menial, aching tasks of daily existence. Chores of self-maintenance such as eating were up to her to take care of. It wasn't enough to eat when fancy struck her; she had to buy, prepare, and cook food EVERY DAY. She often forgot that dishes and cutlery were now her responsibility to clean as well.

Furthermore, it was no longer possible to enjoy the embrace of sleep at one's leisure. It was a DAILY obligation, for six whole, irredeemable hours. She still remembered a time, decades ago, of the world she'd been a part of before the Kingdom. During this time, many experts had recommended that without a gargantuan eight hours a day in slumber, you were doing something horribly wrong and would suffer dire consequences. As such, the joy of her existence was forcibly divided into twenty-four hour chunks, grouped by fleeting weeks, months, years towards death.

Joanne could no longer enjoy life as a never-ending reel, a continuous pursuit of leisure and pleasure fully within her control. She was forced to savour it in fragmented scraps, marred with work, shopping, eating, chores, warding off disease, washing, and other forms of restless responsibility. Bitterly, she lamented the injustice of it all. Would you make a jigsaw of the *Mona Lisa*? Why not take a sledgehammer to Michelangelo's *David* and marvel at the masterpiece one crumbled fragment at a time? Such was the indignity of a sleep forced upon her.

Was it really so bad? Michael had always accused her of being melodramatic. Then again, he wasn't down here to live through this. She thought of Michael, her husband of so many decades... did this punishment serve to settle the score between them? She wondered if they would ever be able to forgive each other.

She walked outside, looked upwards towards the underbelly of the Kingdom. It arched over the entirety of the Underneath like a colossal spider, at once providing protection and damnation, itself shrouded in the darkness of distance. Looking back down, she saw a supporting pillar rooted like a tree trunk at the end of the street, coinciding with the districts outer border.

This curious structure pulsated as though alive with the tiny machines working to repair it, to guard it against entropy.

Not so long ago her flesh had been maintained against injury and the ravages of time. Now, after just a few days, watching the pillar self repair in the same way made her skin crawl.

Looking over the formidable 30 foot sheet of steel forming

the district border, she saw a torrential downpour in the outer world leading to a swallowing darkness. It had been almost a hundred years since she'd originally joined the Kingdom, and she found it hard to remember the outside world. Would it bear much resemblance to the world she'd left behind? So far, a sound had never crossed the border. Instinctively, she imagined acid rains, the blasted skin of a polluted landscape.

It was exhausting to think about. Across the street, a bustling bar beckoned with brilliant light. If nothing else, a few drinks would soothe the sinewy pain in her shoulder, so she made her way inside.

On adjusting to the glaring light, Joanne found an unusual warmth and comfort beating through the heart of her new surroundings. The oak beams and plush reds of the pub were jovial and full of life, a surprising pulse of personality in an otherwise deadened concrete landscape.

Clusters of wasteful individuals knocked back cheap drinks whilst laughing and shooting pool, their stink of mortality permeating the bar. Joanne kept to herself and found a quiet stool at the far end of the counter, keeping her eyes downcast.

The bar-tender watched her intently. Perhaps he thought her beautiful despite her melancholy, or because of it, and fancied his chances. Just as likely, he understood her story and sympathised with her, as with many of his patrons.

"Hey there. You're new down here? I can tell."

"Huh?"

"You look as though this world will never be enough."

"It doesn't matter." Joanne replied dismissively, glancing up only briefly. He was tall, and whilst not handsome per-say he clearly took care of himself. That must be tough in a world like this, she thought.

"No? I guess not. I've not been down here too long to be honest. I'm still figuring things out, but life with the implants already feels like a dream, pleasant, but too unreal." He spoke softly and wistfully, with a deep, comforting voice like brown sugar. "I'm Jim." He extended a strong, welcoming hand, smirking warmly. Joanne's felt like a kitten's paw as she accepted his handshake, tried to relax.

"Joanne."

"So, what brings you down here?"

"I got pregnant. It was an accident, though I thought I'd be able to get away with it if I hid it well enough."

Jim drew back, his eyes widened.

"You're pregnant? I'll have to cut you off..." He took her whiskey away.

"I'm sure it wouldn't have survived my leaving the Kingdom. Besides, who would start a family in a place like this?"

"Why do you say that? You're not the only one who got pregnant up there, and even afterwards the pregnancies have gone fine. People can and do start families down here. A nice couple came in here the other day with a baby; they're applying for an outer-world permit next year."

"What permit?"

"Yeah an outer-world permit. That's what you need to get out of here. Not that I can tell if it's any better than here, from what I've heard nobody ever comes back. Anyway, how far along are you?"

"I'm not sure... can't be too far along." Joanne reasoned that her implants would have let the Kingdom know at the first sign of pregnancy.

Jim nodded, understanding the whole process as little as she did. Some bio-feedback data was always checked up above, though it was hard to know what was examined exactly. The implants now being inactive, it seemed so unusual that they had entrusted their wellbeing to technology they'd never fully understood. He slipped her a card.

"Here's the number for the women's shelter around the corner. You'll get through this."

Momentarily, she felt a grumble of pain. Clutching her stomach, she realised that she'd once again forgotten to eat, and wondered when and if she'd ever adjust to her new needs. Jim was quick to notice:

"Please, get something from the menu for yourself as well. I always help newcomers."

"Mm, thank you!" For the first time since her exile Joanne cracked the faintest smile.

Jim was still watching her: "Your husband's welcome too of course... if he's with you."

Joanne took a deep breath, unsure if she was willing to deal with the topic right now.

"I suppose not..." Jim trailed off.

"No he's not here." Joanne blurted, averting her gaze. "He's not the father." In truth, Joanne wasn't sure who was. It was a moment of drunken weakness on a night out, of indulgence which had become more and more common in the Kingdom. Amongst the implants was one prompting infertility, but or whatever reason hers had become disabled without her knowledge. There hadn't been any opportunity to investigate how or why.

Joanne glanced around the bar; somehow expecting to recognise a face she couldn't remember amongst the crowd. Who knows, she might meet the father again someday, down here.

"Oh, I'm sorry for the intrusion. It's really none of my business." Jim smiled sheepishly, as Joanne silently perused the menu.

Michael beamed joyously, basking in instant gratification as he played the grand piano in his living room. Jaunty notes enchanted the air, reverberated off the polished marble furniture, and caressed the white leather sofa, soaking in to the luxurious comfort of the carpet. Everything was perfect.

He was glad he'd decided to download mastery of the grand piano. The Kingdom had suggested it some time ago. Was it last month? Last year? How many times had the sun come and gone in the decades he and Joanne had spent together, no line or wrinkle lasting for more than a second?

They'd met when The Kingdom had come into its own. By the time they'd married, implants had been created to repair, nourish, inform and entertain them. They were prepared for a life above, together. Decades must have passed.

Then, he was alone with nothing more than his own music for company. Joanne hated the piano, wouldn't have let him indulge himself, but she was gone now. It was fine, having no audience outside of whoever he fancied popping in. It was better that way, he told himself.

What day was it? Instantaneously with his asking the question, almost unconsciously and imperceptibly, the Kingdom granted Michael the answer. Wednesday, 3:59pm. Did it matter? No bedtime was approaching; Michael hadn't chosen to sleep in three years. He preferred to spend his eternity in the study of art, philosophy, culture, history, or anything his heart desired. Often times he would download entire anthologies, collections of academia to peruse at leisure. Just two sundowns ago he accessed the entire works of Charles Bukowski and spent a while mulling them over, like dissolving a chocolate in his mouth.

Mmm, chocolate. No, sweet potato fries! Gammon and fried eggs! Michael drifted into the dining room as he pondered his desire. The Kingdom beamed in his meal of gammon which he ate slowly as usual, savouring for the sake of savouring as he lazily admired the view outside. Drifting off, he accidentally impaled his finger, but felt no pain. The implants repaired him in a second, leaving no sign but a drop of blood on his plate.

Later, he mused that he might idly stroll through the streets, observing his fellow citizens. Or perhaps he could scroll through the details of whatever characters took his interest, as their various personal profiles popped up in front of him. Nah, he decided, he'd done enough of that. The streets were emptier these days.

He stared through the window, admiring a perfect sunset. The apartment was on the edge of the Kingdom, so he could see transport ships headed to the Underneath. More citizens had been sent downwards as of late. Asking the Kingdom by merely forming the query in his mind, he was told that the remaining population was only a few thousand. The crimes committed for exile were typically petty theft, vandalism, small time violence and the like.

Drifting to the window, he was reminded of the other common reason for exile, one still so fresh in his mind. Looking out, he saw another couple led out from their apartment across the street, trying to comfort one another as they were shoved towards a transport. He could only assume that the couple had fallen pregnant. News headlines had reported on the issue months ago. It appeared that information had been leaked from the higher ups working to maintain the Kingdom. They'd found a way to control the characteristics of their implants, and remove the chemical imbalances causing infertility. It still begged the question, why? Why fight to ensure your own damnation? Joanne, of all people, along with the bastard she'd slept with...

"Why?" he asked himself aloud, summoning a glass of fine wine into his hand with an ethereal glow. "Why has such stupidity gripped the people?"

The transport plunged downwards like an elevator, removing the offenders from this world. Breathing deeply, Michael knocked back his glass in one powerful, frustrated movement. Marching away from the scene, he slumped onto his couch and demanded everything from the Kingdom. Everything there was to know about the world below.

In an instant, he learned of life in the Underneath, that its people had rediscovered their humanity. They struggled, felt pain and fatigue alongside joy, the full experience of life. He was shocked and confused to find that, after only a short while of yearning to return, many of them were excited to head in to the wider world.

How unusual. Trying to understand it gave him a headache. He ran his hands through his hair, pacing through his house in search of some distraction. He felt the first wave of restlessness, of frustration that he'd experienced in decades. Uncertain of how to express this and cope with it, he found the first object he could think of - his so recently precious piano - and smashed upon it in an awful, jarring, piercing set of notes. Summoning a sledgehammer, he crashed upon it in a short-lived expression of chaos. To his chagrin, tiny machines repaired it to its former state in an instant. Dropping the sledgehammer in disgust, he stormed outside.

In years past, Michael had always been charmed by the appearance chosen for the Kingdom. He'd originally imagined that it would be constructed in the image of heaven, with pearly white columns and cloudy landscapes. Instead, it had been modelled after 1950s American suburbia, the white picket-fence and apple pie stereotype. At least, that was the model for this section, where the two of them had chosen to live together. Further, alternative selections for an ideal lifestyle spread for miles into the distance, each like sections of a spider's web. Somewhere in the centre of it all was the nucleus of the community, a building housing a vast supercomputer hidden from public view and understanding. In that moment, he appreciated how this world was only as real as the intelligence which had created it.

Seeing a few satisfied citizens on a stroll, he knew he'd never forge a true connection with any of them. Their presence suddenly seemed no greater than figures on a cinema screen, playing ultimately meaningless roles. Despite all the possibilities his life yielded to him, there were none worth pursuing without her. Amidst the coursing monotony, this was all he knew.

As Joanne's meal was placed unceremoniously before her, she realised she'd never been so hungry. She'd almost forgotten the sensation over so many years, having merely allowed herself to feel peckish. This ravenous hunger was a new rumble, a new experience.

Steak and ale pie with buttery shortbread pastry, smooth mashed potatoes, crisp and fresh garden peas, complete with lashings of rich, warm onion gravy. Such simple food had never before tasted so complex. Somehow, despite years of eating whatever her heart had desired back in the Kingdom, nothing had tasted finer and no greater jolts of pleasure had gone through her than at that moment, devouring a modest meal in a small bar in the Underneath.

Her shoulder still throbbed with pain, but at least now she was able to block some of it out. She glanced up at Jim, they shared an awkward smile.

"Is everything ok?" He asked, scratching behind his ear. She didn't respond at first. There was something so familiar about the way he scratched like that. Suddenly, he seemed like an old friend, someone she'd met before. All things considered, maybe they had. She'd forgotten that, although a lot of the patrons seemed like louts, they'd once been members of the above world just as much as she had. Everyone was in this together.

"It's great, thanks. Say..." She looked up smiling, speaking sweetly "What did you do with yourself, when you were still in the Kingdom?"

"Me? Heh, not much of anything truth be told. Looking back, I sometimes wish I'd done more, but I spent most of my time just heading out and getting drunk. It wasn't like we'd get hungover, was it? Haha, maybe the reason I don't miss it all that much is because I don't remember too much of it! Going out with my friends, meeting all sorts of girls. Then one day about a week ago, they just escorted me down. The whole thing was so rushed they wouldn't even tell me what I'd done. 'You broke the rules.' They said. Total injustice."

"I see. You just seem kinda familiar is all. Sometimes I just had to get away from my husband. Maybe the two of us bumped into each other once!"

"And here we are again. It's a small world, isn't it?"

The two laughed, looking in to each other's eyes.

No longer was she afraid and exhausted, the nagging splinter felt in her old life having been tweaked at last. That fleeting moment she'd had locking eyes with her husband of eighty years, laughing together one day, she hadn't been able to ignore that yearning dullness, that sense of desperation.

She recalled the day she'd confessed to Michael. She remembered how his dullness had persisted, with a somehow greater fire than that of actual rage, an emotional disconnect more horrible than passionate anger.

"You'll be exiled from the Kingdom." Michael had announced flatly. The burn of betrayal, the shaking of sorrow that he should have felt had been extracted by the comforts of their 'perfect' lifestyle. She knew she'd lost him years ago; these words merely set it in stone. He'd become addicted to the instant gratification of his every whim, at the cost of everything. The fire in his eyes. Their burning love for one another. The man she'd known, when they'd wrestled through a life of poverty, when he'd held her hands and promised her everything in the world. Was there anything left of those promises?

"Michael, I'm sorry. I don't even know where to begin. But still..." she trailed, tenderly, her voice wavering. "Don't you care? Doesn't this make you feel anything? Anything at all?"

His eyes, once bright, had sunk like doused campfires in the outline of his face. His strong jaw, once clenched with ambition, thought only of his next whim.

"They already know. They're on their way. You'll just have to live on the Underneath. You knew the rules."

Immediately, an awful knock pounded at their door. Robotic and unhesitant, Michael had walked over and let the officers in. It had been like an assembly line, the way those men in uniform clutched her arms in a vice-grip, bashing her shoulder against the door-frame as they led her out in to the street.

"MICHAEL!!"

Michael watched from the doorway, like he'd turned away an unwanted salesman. Before she'd even stopped struggling, he closed the door behind him.

Joanne trembled at the bar, having only just allowed herself to fully register the last week with a glass of lemonade to her lips. Reflexively, she smashed the glass on to the counter, where it roared fragments of glass like broken dreams across the bar. The faces around her grew a little sullen, but they understood. A few mouthed "newcomer" to one another. Jim swept up the glass, not breathing a word.

Eventually, she forced herself to calm down. The bar's activity continued, and she did her best to compose herself as a few other patrons gave her concerned looks. If nothing else, she tried to appreciate the solidarity. The challenges of this new world were still overwhelming, but at least she no longer felt quite so alone.

Joanne grew accustomed to the bar and her new home as the days passed. As she grew closer to Jim, the nagging feeling of familiarity lingered, of some drunken night lost from memory.

It was late one night, almost closing time, as Joanne and Jim were the only two left in the bar. She chatted to him cheerfully as he tidied up. By now, she'd almost grown used to the world, and what happiness it had to offer.

The door swung open, and an old face entered the bar. One she'd hoped never to see again, even if he'd given up everything to find her, to win her back. Michael.

She sprang to her feet in rage and repulsion, ready to act somewhere between the two. Michael took a step towards her, finding himself at a loss for words, as Jim stayed close to her, holding her back.

She struggled for a second, and then... there was something even more familiar about him and the way he smelled, how he held her.

That was when it clicked. Memories returned of that night, going somewhere alone together.

The three of them realised together. Michael looked for one last time upon his former wife and the father of her child as, with silent tears of loss; he backed out of the bar and in to the lonely darkness of the Underneath.

THE END

AUTHOR BIOGRAPHIES
& STORY NOTES

Aizuddin H. Anuar is a writer from Pahang, Malaysia. Currently, his writing focuses on the interrelated themes of memory, identity, migration and family. His works of fiction have been featured in *BFM: The Business Station*, *Odd One Out* magazine, *Eksentrika*, *The Mekong Review*, and anthologies *Endings & Beginnings* and *Telltale Food*.

Why I wrote this story: "This story was inspired by my time in Australia, fashioned as a series of fictional letters about the urgency to leave nothing unsaid prior to impending departure. It fits the theme by chronicling the passage of time in Adam's life, from arrival to Australia until the departure from life itself."

A mythology nut and whisky enthusiast, **C. B. Blakey** lives in England with his wife, his daughter, and enough books to build a small fort. He writes fantasy and light horror short stories and will be starting a novel once he figures out how to fit a few extra hours into the day. His work has appeared in *Metaphorosis* magazine, and in the OWC anthologies *Debut* and *Oxford's Haunted*.

Why I wrote this story: "This story was inspired by the static I heard in my earphones at work and the old myths of the selkie. I think there are a lot of people who would like to just stop work and go to the beach, whether they are a seal-person or not."

'Doc' David was impressed by 'Service of All the Dead', an early episode of *Inspector Morse*, and thought that Oxford looked a nice place to be. Years later he finds himself living here.

Why I wrote this story: "'This Song Is All About War' builds on characters explored in stories I contributed to previous OWC anthologies. The pub, The Anchor, doesn't exist, but something very much like it does. Or did."

Sam Derby lives in South Oxford with his wife Caroline and daughter Hattie. He has never managed to leave Oxford for long since arriving there about twenty-five years ago.

Why I wrote this story: "I had heard the claims of the Queen's Lane and Grand Cafes to be the oldest in England, and when I researched this I got completely engrossed. This gave me the material for a story of arrivals and departure."

Gerlinde De Ryck is a Belgian illustrator. She has a few projects going at the moment, including two children's books and three graphic novels. She also writes an online comic about her partner Thomas at www.thomaszijnstrip.com. In May 2018 she became the mother of a gorgeous daughter, Maren.

Why I wrote this story: "The twenty autobiographical comics in this anthology are based on sketches I made during my pregnancy. I decided to focus on the small, light-hearted moments that might otherwise be forgotten amongst the vast range of emotions that come with expecting a child."

At the time of writing, **Adam Fields** was an active member of the Oxford Writing Circle. After leaving the city for Japan in late 2019, he has since returned to his home town of Sheffield to complete an MA, and procrastinate, perpetually.

Why I wrote this story: "I wanted to put a lens on two people from different parts of society: one that's always departing, looking towards the next opportunity, and the other, a constant; chance encounters can leave enormous impressions, particularly when they remind you to never judge a book by its cover."

Jess Kershaw is an editor based in London. She enjoys writing, and reading, stories about badass women and the natural world

Why I wrote this story: "'When You look into Darkness' is a story I wrote after reading about humans domesticating the first wolves — we really do have an uncanny ability to make friends with our predators. It's an exploration into how far these pack-bonding interests stretch — all the way into the realms of the eldritch abomination, in this case!"

Isabel Galwey graduated from St Hilda's College, Oxford University in 2019, where she studied Chinese. In 2020, she was shortlisted for the Penguin WriteNow programme. She recently said goodbye to Oxford and began her postgraduate studies in Hong Kong.

Why I wrote this story: "'Departures' and 'arrivals' are words which we associate with the process of moving through space. I decided to mix things up slightly and write a story about travelling through time. This story follows one woman as she arrives for work at the world's first time-travel corporation, Kronos

Carole Scott joined the OWC in 2016 and one of her stories was published in the group's first anthology, *Debut*. She published her first novel, *The Broken Heart Repair Plan*, in 2015.

Why I wrote this story: "I've had many bad dates in my life and I have long wanted to depict some of the funnier aspects in a short story. I wanted to find a way to mix the humour and pain that comes from the dating scene and combine it with something darker, more twisted."

Elaine Roberts studied English Literature at Exeter and now works as a marketer in academic publishing. She loves long walks, good food and writing short stories. Often found staring out of the window.

Why I wrote this story: "Most of today's 'window smashing' stunts use CGI, but I've often wondered about the person whose job it once was to create and install false glass. Why pick that role? Did they ever mess up and have to make a new pane? And what if someone held a serious grudge?"

Ian Robertson is a biochemist with literary aspirations and dangerous ideas.

Why I wrote this story: "This science fiction story is inspired by the sense of foreboding sometimes created by travel and technology, as well as an unnatural fascination with pigeons."

Abigail B. Vint has spent over twenty years playing with words professionally. She uses writing to explore our deepest and closest relationships. The Bar was written with her late father in mind, Ralph Vint, who always had a way of making people in his presence feel special. Her short stories have been published in anthologies by the Oxford Writing Circle and Didcot Writers. A dual Canadian-Irish citizen, she lives in Oxford with her partner, David.

Why I wrote this story: "A few chance encounters at a local watering hole reveals more than the patrons expected. But they can always count on the trusty bartender Ralph to fix them a good drink, make them feel comfortable and send them on their way content. He may even eventually find some peace himself."

Alexander Walker occasionally writes short stories, draws pictures, and designs anthology book covers.

Why I wrote this story: "This story came from the idea of souls departing our world and what might arrive in their stead, only, what arrives is not always what was intended."

Alex Ware is an IT professional, former tefl "teacher", writer and beer drinker, currently working and studying in Oxford. He is hoping to improve his craft.

Why I wrote this story: "In 'The Underneath' the protagonist is exiled from a technological paradise, arriving in the 'hell' of the real world. It explores the grumbling dissatisfaction and boredom we often feel in our privileged lives."

ABOUT THE

OXFORD WRITING CIRCLE

The Oxford Writing Circle is one of Oxford's largest and most vibrant writing communities. Its aim is simple: to encourage more people to write because through writing you can make anything. The group organises weekly events, including sessions to gain feedback on current projects, live writing workshops, guest speakers, and socials.

Find out more at oxfordwritingcircle.org.uk and on Meetup.

Lightning Source UK Ltd.
Milton Keynes UK
UKHW040625010221
378041UK00001B/17